What Alan Kincaid is wishing for:

1. A way to get that darn lamp back.

2. A way to convince Gina Cox that his intentions are honorable—even if he did sort of lie about the lamp.

3. A way to convince *himself* that he'll be satisfied with just one kiss from this woman. Really.

What Gina Cox is wishing for:

1. A way to get Alan Kincaid off her back.

2. A way to convince him that she will not be swayed by sweet talk, sweet candy or his big, brown eyes.

3. A way to convince *herself* that he couldn't *possibly* be as perfect as he seems....

Dear Reader,

I think we all remember the story of Aladdin and his lamp, and I'm willing to bet we've all had a few moments in life when we wished we owned that lamp. Really, how hard would it be for me to become tall, thin and so gorgeous that the man of my dreams (who keeps changing on an almost-daily basis, of course) couldn't possibly resist me? Impossible without the lamp, but with it…? Who knows! In Alice Sharpe's *If Wishes Were Heroes* there is indeed such a lamp, or at least there seems to be. Whether it's magical or not, it certainly succeeds in bringing Gina Cox and Alan Kincaid together, and isn't that really the point?

Popular Christie Ridgway is back with *Have Baby, Will Marry*. All Molly Michaels set out to find was a dog. Her friends were all having babies, but for Molly, playing single mom to a cuddly canine was enough. Until she discovered that said canine came attached to gorgeous Weaver Reed and tiny, adorable Daisy. Suddenly, walking the dog looked a whole lot less appealing than walking straight into Weaver's embrace—marriage-of-convenience proposal and all!

I think you're going to love both these books, and I hope you'll rejoin us next month for two more lighthearted tales about unexpectedly meeting, dating—and marrying!—Mr. Right.

Leslie Wainger
Senior Editor and Editorial Coordinator

Please address questions and book requests to:
Silhouette Reader Service
U.S.: 3010 Walden Ave., P.O. Box 1325, Buffalo, NY 14269
Canadian: P.O. Box 609, Fort Erie, Ont. L2A 5X3

ALICE SHARPE

If Wishes Were Heroes

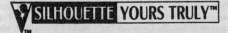

SILHOUETTE YOURS TRULY™

Published by Silhouette Books

America's Publisher of Contemporary Romance

This book is dedicated with oodles of love to
Katherine Alice Jones, in appreciation of her smiles.

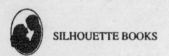 SILHOUETTE BOOKS

ISBN 0-373-52052-2

IF WISHES WERE HEROES

Books by Alice Sharpe

Silhouette Yours Truly

If Wishes Were Heroes

Silhouette Romance

Going to the Chapel #1137
Missing: One Bride #1212

1

REWARD!!! plus expenses for return of Aladdin-like brass lamp mistakenly sold at garage sale, August 15, 482 Hazelnut Way. Family keepsake. Call 555-1000.

Gina Cox folded the classified section of the newspaper down on itself, recalling the day two weeks earlier when she and Howard Raskeller, a man she was by then sure *wasn't* the love of her life, had visited a garage sale on Hazelnut Way. Her gaze traveled to a pile of unpacked boxes heaped in one corner of her brand-new office. Buried in one of those boxes was the lamp she'd purchased that day, the lamp she'd been so delighted to find as it fit the decor of a restaurant she was in the process of decorating...the lamp it now seemed she must return.

"Drat." She sighed, running a hand through the wavy mass of bronze curls that fell to her shoulders. Glancing at her watch, Gina found she had a spare two hours before a scheduled appointment with a troublesome client. Digging through the boxes might at least take her mind off a visit that was sure to prove irritating—at best. The thought did flit through her mind that she didn't need to return the lamp—it was hers, free and clear to do with as she pleased. In the end, however, it was the phrase "family keepsake" that kept repeating in her head.

In the bottom layer of the second-to-last box, she finally hit pay dirt. As she freed the lamp from a bed of tissue paper, Gina was once again delighted by the graceful contours, the curved spout, the etched lotus blossom base, the rich patina. She recalled how her little decorator's heart had beat faster when she saw the sticker on the base—five dollars. She would have paid ten times that much!

What an odd little ornament to be called a family keepsake. Biting her lip, Gina tried to imagine the story behind it. A sweet old man had sold it to her— had he bought it as a keepsake of a romantic adventure in the Middle East? Maybe it went back further than him, back to a soldier grandfather who had discovered it in a bazaar and brought it home along with tales of heroics that cemented the lamp as a keepsake. Or perhaps it was owned by a great-aunt who had married a sultan and used the lamp, burning oil, to read and reread letters from home.

Speculation and fancy aside, in some way, this lamp was connected to a family who cared enough to cast a net for its return.

Keepsakes were not a matter Gina took lightly. Abandoned at birth by a young and unmarried mother, Gina had been raised by her maternal grandparents. Grandfather was a tough old cookie who refused to even hear his wayward daughter's name spoken in his presence. Grandmother was softer but just as reticent about discussing the past. Gina had one memento, a silver locket her mother had worn when she was a girl. A worthless little object to most, the locket was invaluable to Gina. No doubt about it, she understood the true importance of a keepsake!

Of course, the owner of the Mediterranean restaurant she was decorating might not feel quite as benevolent as Gina when he learned she'd given back the lamp she'd described to him in such glowing detail. But she'd deal with him later.

As she dialed the number in the paper, she took a cursory glance at the desk clock and gasped. Where had the time gone? She slammed down the receiver, grabbed her briefcase and her roomy black purse, tossing the lamp inside the bag at the last second. She could return it in person if the appointment with Julia Ann Dunsberry didn't run too long.

Three hours later, exhausted but relieved to have the Dunsberry visit over for another week, Gina pulled her car to a stop in front of 482 Hazelnut Way. The house was two stories of brown shingles, the trim painted forest green, the yard bordered with a picket fence. A maple tree, leaves turning gold, occupied one corner of the lot; a rope swing dangled from a low branch, inviting a person to sit on the wooden seat and laze away a September afternoon. Though a good deal more modest than the estate she'd just visited, this house looked homey and warm.

A long porch graced the front. As Gina walked up a broad flight of stairs and crossed to the door, she found herself forming a mental picture of the people who lived here. One was a given, the older man who had sold her the lamp. He'd have a cozy wife. The furniture would be pieces collected over a long marriage, oak, perhaps, braided rugs, tweed upholstery, potted plants.

The door flew inward when she rapped on it, and she heard a far-off voice call from deep inside. She barely made out an invitation to enter.

Hooking her bag over her shoulder, she stepped inside and closed the door behind her, then turned to face the living room. It was much as she had imagined, except for the ten-speed bike pushed up against one wall and stacks of magazines and books piled on the large coffee table.

The smell of cookies—so right for this house—filled the air.

"I'm back here in the kitchen," a voice called. "Aren't you early? Damn!"

The oath, on the other hand, didn't fit. It was quickly followed by a loud clattering sound, which effectively ended the one-sided conversation and led Gina down a short hall that erupted into a kitchen, a small square room with late-afternoon sunshine streaming through large windows.

Standing in the middle of the room, in front of an open oven, was a man wearing an apron and an oven mitt. The apron was bright red and printed on it in white letters were the words Kiss the Cook. An aluminum cookie tray lay at his feet, and what appeared to be a dozen broken sugar cookies were scattered across the floor in front of him. At the sound of Gina's footsteps, he looked up.

Mischievous brown eyes closed the distance between them, eyes with challenging glints in their mahogany depths. Vaguely, Gina was aware of the rest of him, the high cheekbones, the straight dark brows, the black hair that flopped over his forehead, the size and breadth of his lean, muscular body, the faded blue jeans, the brown leather boots. But it was his eyes that held her.

They never left her face as he closed the oven door with his foot and picked up the cookie tray, setting it in the sink. "Tell me you're not Naomi Roberts here to collect cookies for the bake sale," he said.

The intensity of his gaze had dazzled Gina. She blinked to break the trance. "I'm not Naomi Roberts," she told him.

"Good. I seem to be having a problem in the baking department. Anyway, I didn't think you were. I hear she has five kids and she's plump."

"I don't have five kids," Gina told him.

"No, I don't imagine you do. And you're not plump, either." This last remark was followed by a lingering once-over, which Gina knew took in her trim charcoal suit, silver earrings and locket and black pumps. She'd dressed conservatively that morning, knowing she'd need a businesslike air to cope with Julia Ann's flights of fancy. So, why did she suddenly wish she'd chosen something frilly and frivolous?

"Don't tell me who you are," he commanded, his eyes dancing.

"Why not?"

"Because I know."

She glanced down at her purse, sure the lamp must be peeking a spout through an open zipper, but the bag was closed and the lamp was completely hidden.

"Okay, I'll bite," she said, playing along. "Who am I?"

He leaned back against the counter. "You've got to be with the cookie police," he said with a grin.

Gina laughed softly. "Actually—"

"Wait a second. Before you place me under arrest, I think you should know there are extenuating circumstances you may not have considered."

A charmer, that's what he was, a charmer. Well, Gina thought to herself, she had just recently tangled with a charmer and look where it had landed her: out of an office, nursing a major case of wounded pride and a minor broken heart. On the other hand, this man was just an acquaintance; if she started using Howard Raskeller as a yardstick by which to measure every man she met, she'd spend the rest of her life avoiding the male gender. She smiled and said, "Okay, I'll bite, what are the extenuating circumstances?"

He took off the oven mitt and held it in front of his face. Gina could actually see his eyes sparkle through the three big holes in the fabric. "I burned myself on the cookie sheet."

Two could play this game. "Sorry, but equipment failure doesn't relieve you of responsibility for the crime," she said, adding as she gestured at the floor, "there's just so much evidence piled up against you."

He shook his head. "Geez, you're tough."

"Tough? What about that apron? Kiss the Cook?"

"Soliciting, huh?"

She shrugged.

Looking straight into her eyes, he said, "Maybe it's just wishful thinking."

Just as she thought! A total charmer.

"Wait," he said, moving suddenly. From the space between the refrigerator and the wall, he pulled a broom with a dustpan stuck on the handle. As he swept, he cast her a smug grin.

Gina folded her arms across her chest. "I must warn you, tampering with the evidence—"

"What evidence?" he interrupted as he swept the cookie crumbs into the dustpan. He dumped the "evidence" into the garbage under the sink and tossed the broom back beside the refrigerator, where it banged against the wall. Then he tore off the apron, revealing a black T-shirt faded to gray, a T-shirt that had probably shrunk in a too-hot dryer and that now molded the tantalizing muscles of his chest and upper arms.

Worse than she thought! This guy was charming *and* gorgeous. Gina bit her bottom lip and averted her gaze. "I guess you're off the hook," she mumbled.

"Whew! For a minute there I was beginning to think I was going to be locked away for good. Okay, now, what's your name?"

"Gina Cox."

"Nice to meet you, Gina. I'm Alan Kincaid. So, if you don't mind my asking, why did you waltz into my kitchen?"

Gina's mission came flooding back to her. "Actually, I'm looking for the older man who lives in this house."

"You want Uncle Joe," he stated, adding with a grin, "which wounds me."

She wanted to tell him he could stop flirting, it wasn't going to work on her. She said, "It's just that I have his brass lamp—"

Alan abruptly crossed the few feet between them and clasped her arms in a pair of very strong hands. "You? You're the one who bought the lamp?"

This position brought them close to an embrace, something he seemed to notice at the same time Gina did. He released her and took a step back. "You just have no idea what it's been like around here since Uncle Joe sold that trinket in his garage sale along with the rest of our junk."

Gina had been in the process of unzipping her purse when his words stopped her. She turned bewildered eyes toward him. "Trinket? The ad said it was a family keepsake."

"Of course it is," he said quickly.

Somewhat mollified, she began digging for the lamp. "I wish he was here," she admitted as her fingers closed around the cool metal. "I'd love to know how he came to sell something that is obviously so important to him."

"Actually, it's mine," Alan said, his features softening as she produced the lamp. "Uncle Joe held the sale while I was away for a week doing a job up north in Seattle. He was trying to raise enough money to—well, never mind. Anyway, when I found out about it, I'm the one who advertised to get it back. I have to admit I thought the chances were slim that whoever bought it would read my ad."

"I'm a decorator by profession," she explained. "I always read the yard sale column in the Friday paper. It was clever of you to place your plea there." She turned the lamp over in her hands much as she had earlier in the day. "It almost looks as though there should be a genie inside this thing," she mused.

He looked startled. More than startled, perhaps. Alarmed.

"Look at the way it's been rubbed on the right side," she added.

The alarmed expression gave way to one of amusement. "Well, go on, make a wish."

"No—" she protested.

"Why not? You don't believe in genies, do you?"

"Of course not."

"Then, make a wish."

Without warning, Gina thought of the mother she'd never known. She shook her head.

"Come on," Alan coaxed.

"This is silly."

"Humor me."

They exchanged a drawn-out look that defied explanation. As much to break the spell of their silence as to indulge him, she gave in. "Why not?" *But not a wish for my mom.* A moment of thought was followed by a low chuckle. "This is so unlikely it can't possibly happen without magical intervention."

"The best kind of wish."

"Okay, here goes. I wish Julia Ann Dunsberry would stop following me around her house, 'helping' me work. The woman drives me crazy." Gina rubbed the lamp vigorously, closing her eyes as she did so. For a second, it seemed as though she was tumbling, but only inside her head. Dizziness, she decided, because she'd skipped lunch to search for the lamp. She opened her eyes and found Alan smiling at her.

Her cheeks suddenly felt hot, as if she'd been caught doing something illicit. "That's enough of that," she warned him.

"Sorry. You just looked so...earnest. Who is this Julia Ann?"

"A genuine southern belle married to a very proper, very British gent who counts on me to temper his wife's more outrageous ideas. This is growing increasingly difficult."

"Ah. Well, now you're going to have to get back to me and let me know if the magic worked."

She smiled patiently. Sure...she'd get back to him...right around the time she decided she was ripe for another trip through the ego smasher. He looked more than able to break a heart or two before lunch.

"How much did Uncle Joe charge you for the lamp?"

"Five dollars," she told him as she handed the lamp over. When he took it, their fingers brushed. Well, she'd delivered the lamp back to its owner. It was time to hit the road, and yet she realized she was sorry to leave the lamp behind. It wasn't as though she'd ever entertained the idea of keeping it for herself, so why did she feel so reluctant to part with it?

"About the reward—"

"No reward," she interrupted, but the streak of curiosity resurfaced. "However, I *do* have a question I'd like answered."

"You want to know why a hunk like me is baking cookies?" he said with a chuckle. "I'm not normally so domestic, but the Roberts woman left a message on the machine—apparently Sara forgot to warn me she needed cookies today. Maybe she told Rob or Uncle Joe, which is about as effective as whistling into the wind. Anyway, I thought, what the heck, I'm home early, I'll bake them! As you know, it didn't exactly work out.''

''That's not what I wanted to know,'' she said, wondering who on earth all the people he'd mentioned were.

''Oh. Then you want to know if I'm married. Not me. No time, no inclination, no way!''

''There's a huge surprise,'' she muttered.

He narrowed his eyes. ''What does *that* mean?''

She'd been about to point out that his easy way with a strange woman who popped unannounced into his kitchen precluded a serious ongoing relationship, but how did she know that? ''You're not wearing a wedding ring,'' she said diplomatically.

''Neither are you,'' he said.

''You bet I'm not. I'm through with men.''

This comment caused his eyebrows to inch up his forehead. ''Do I detect the singed fingers of someone caught playing with matches?''

''If you're trying to ask if I've been burned by a man, the answer is yes, who hasn't?''

''Ouch!''

Gina realized a little late she'd gotten carried away. ''Sorry.''

''No offense taken, not much, anyway. Okay, back to your question. I'm twenty-nine years old, own a small electrical contracting business, employ three other guys who hang on my every word, I have never been convicted of a felony—''

Gina suppressed a smile and shook her head.

Both hands held palm upward, he said, ''I give up.''

Her voice turned serious. "It's the lamp. I'd like to know in what way it's a family keepsake."

He nodded, but for once seemed short of words. Gina waited for an explanation, her imagination once again running away in a land of minarets....

Alan Kincaid looked down at the very lovely, very expectant face of the woman standing in front of him and tried to figure out what to say. Never in his wildest dreams had he imagined anyone would actually ask this question, yet now that this beauty had, it seemed only logical. When he'd placed the ad in the paper, he'd tacked on the words "family keepsake" at the last moment because without them, the ad had seemed impersonal and extremely unlikely to bring the lamp back.

Trouble was, Sara had sworn him to secrecy, making him promise not to divulge to *anyone* who really wanted the lamp, and especially not *why!* So what did he do now? Break his promise to Sara so he wouldn't look like a creep to Gina? He hated to do that; he'd given his word, and in his book, that meant something. That left making up a story Gina would believe and hoping she would never mention it again.

Wait, why did it matter what he told her? She was a stranger who would walk out of his life the second her curiosity was satisfied! This thought produced an inward groan as he acknowledged to himself the fact that he'd been talking a blue streak since the first second he saw Gina precisely because he didn't want her to leave.

It had been so long since he'd been attracted to a woman, and never like this, never at first sight. Most likely his wild attempts at humor had seemed more like bigheaded bravado to her. Bottom line—hurry, think quick, come up with something to say.

Gina apparently got tired of waiting for him. Glancing without guile from beneath thick lashes, she said, "Has it been in your family a long time?"

There was such a note of whimsy in her voice he decided on the spot to go along with her. "More or...er...less."

Her smile extended right on up into her eyes. They were an incredible color, like a high bank of clouds before a spring rain. Wishing to dilute his lie with a shot of truth, he added, "My mother died when I was eleven, and my brother, Rob, was less than a year old. After a while, Dad married again, and a few years later they had Sara, who is now thirteen. Then he and his second wife were both killed by a drunk driver three years ago."

This information made Gina's eyes fly open. "Oh, I'm sorry. How dreadful—"

"Yes," he interrupted, sorry he'd burdened her with all this family history, and yet kind of glad, too. Sara's losses helped explain her quirky streak, and her quirky streak was what had landed him in his current predicament. "It's been hard for all of us, especially Sara," he explained. "We're a family, Sara, Rob, Uncle Joe and me. An odd one, maybe, but a complete family, each of us with our own different roles. It's hardest on Sara, though. Losing both her folks at once like that, especially her mom—well, you can't imagine what it was like for her."

He noticed Gina gingerly touch the locket that rested against her white blouse. Then she squared her shoulders beneath her severe jacket, a gesture that left Alan speculating about how she looked without two layers of fabric and a bulky pair of shoulder pads obscuring her shape. Perfect, he'd wager, absolutely perfect.

She cleared her throat. "Was it your mother's lamp, is that it?"

He met her gaze.

She looked instantly contrite. "Forgive me for prying."

"You're not prying," he assured her before he could caution himself to let her think she was prying so she'd stop unintentionally backing him into a corner!

"Was your mother as exotic as her brass lamp?"

Seizing the opportunity to steer the conversation onto safer ground, Alan said, "Mom looked just like that genie on television, only she had a dark ponytail instead of a blond one. Same predilection for filmy veils and sheer pants and showing off her belly button, though."

Her reaction to his latest attempt at humor was to furrow her brow and regard him with a look bordering on disgust. Suddenly, a host of long-forgotten memories hit him so hard it took his breath away, and falteringly, he added, "My mother *was* exotic. She wore...boring clothes, I guess...but I remember almond-shaped black eyes...alabaster skin...a soft voice. She used to sing to me."

The disgusted look fled, but the questions were back. "The lamp passed through her family?"

Ah, geez, this was getting way beyond awkward. "Gina—"

"Wait!" she interrupted. "You're telling me your uncle sold a lamp that had once been your mother's possession? How could he have done that?"

Oh, boy, a new wrinkle. "Well, Uncle Joe isn't the most sentimental of people, and besides, he wanted to go to the track."

Her expression clearly reflected how horrified she was. "He sold something of value to you because he wanted to bet on a horse?"

"No. Well, kind of—"

"Kind of?"

Alan carefully set the lamp on the counter beside him. Enough was enough. He cautiously stepped closer to Gina, reaching out to touch her arm, sensing he'd need to keep tabs on her while he broke his promise to Sara and told Gina the truth. "Listen—" he began, but was cut short by the sound of slamming car doors in the driveway. "Damn. Sara must be home. Gina, really, I'm sorry."

She shook her head. "About what?"

"There isn't time to explain," he said.

She stared at him with questions in her eyes, questions he had waited too long to answer. "Damn," he said again as he dropped his hand.

Gina was confused. Amazingly, the confusion seemed to lessen as Alan stepped away from her and she was suddenly able to take a deep breath. The back door opened abruptly, and in strode a thin teenage girl with long, pale hair, a shopping bag clutched to her chest. A tentative smile died on her lips as she caught sight of Gina. Her gaze immediately dropped to the floor and she continued walking on through the hall door. The whole thing took less than twenty seconds.

"My sister is a little shy," Alan said.

Gina nodded. She thought this observation an understatement.

Next through the door was the older man Gina had last seen at the garage sale.

"Next time that girl needs clothes, *you* go with her," he told Alan. "This was too short and that was too long and another thing that looked like a sack big enough for two or three girls Sara's size was too small..." His voice trailed off as he caught sight of Gina. "I know you," he said. He was built like a bulldog with a barrel chest and short legs. A few gray hairs fringed his ears and neck. "I never forget a face as pretty as yours, but I'm not so good on names."

"This is Gina," Alan said quickly. "Gina, Joe Kincaid."

"We met at your yard sale about two weeks ago," Gina explained. "I'm the one who bought the brass lamp."

"Sure, I remember you."

"Well," Alan said with a deep sigh, "I know you're busy...."

It took Gina a second to realize the remark was addressed to her, a not-so-subtle hint she should leave. She slipped her purse back on her shoulder.

"Hope you don't think I tried to cheat you out of five bucks," Joe said as he shrugged off his sweater and hung it on a peg by the door.

"Well, no," Gina stammered, casting Alan a befuddled glance. He made a move toward the door.

Joe's eyes focused on the counter behind Gina.

"Don't tell me you brought that piece of junk back!" He chortled as he suddenly reached around Gina, hooked a finger through the lamp's handle and swung it in the air. The erratic movement dislodged the lid, which clattered on the linoleum.

Gina was shocked by the older man's lack of respect. She immediately stepped forward and picked up the lid, plucking the lamp from Joe's fingers and cradling it in her hands. "You should be careful with this," she admonished.

He looked genuinely startled by her concern. "Why?"

"Because it's very important to your nephew," she said as she fit the two pieces back together. "A keepsake from his mother, an heirloom, really—"

"Now, wait just a second, missy, you're all mixed up. You tell her, Al, tell her how you found this piece of tin in a box in the Widow Hawking's garage, what was it, a month ago?" Looking at Gina, he added, "Al was rewiring the place for her, said it was a regular firetrap. Anyway, honey, you can see it ain't no heirloom, and it has nothing to do with Al's mother, God rest her soul."

Gina stared at the old man. Eventually, her gaze moved onto Alan, who looked as though he wished a giant hole would open up in the earth and swallow him. She said, "Is this true?"

He tried smiling, but it didn't stick. Finally, he nodded.

Needing to hear it stated clearly, Gina said, "The lamp never belonged to your mother?"

"No," he said stiffly. It seemed to Gina he was on the verge of adding something, but his gaze darted to the hallway and back again. Gina heard a rustling sound and turned to see Sara had come back and was watching the proceedings with round eyes. "No," Alan repeated.

She shoved the lamp into his hands. "So you lied in the newspaper and you lied to my face just because you wanted the lamp back, but you aren't willing to explain?" Part of her was patting herself on the back for being so clever she'd figured out this scheming no-good from the get-go; another part was willing him to explain why he'd let her make a fool of herself over something so inconsequential.

Uncle Joe stuck in his two cents. "Let me get this straight, Al. You lied in the newspaper?"

Alan sighed. "Yes, Uncle Joe, I lied in the newspaper. Don't you know you can't believe everything you read?"

"Oh, brother," Gina said, shaking her head. With one last frown cast in Alan's direction, she exited through the back door. She was a little surprised when he fell into step beside her. They didn't speak until they hit the sidewalk.

"It's all so simple," he said.

She waited as he searched for those supposedly simple words. He threw a few worried looks over his shoulder toward the house, and finally, Gina had had enough.

"I don't think your uncle is going to come running out here to contradict your next story, so go ahead."

"Now, wait a second—"

"I do see your little sister looking out of one of the upstairs windows, however."

He looked toward the top story, where a curtain

was fluttering out through an open window. Sara was no longer there. When he turned back to Gina, he shook his head. "You're just going to have to trust me," he said softly.

"Trust you? Why in the world should I trust you? You're a liar, Alan Kincaid, and if you lie so easily about the little things, you probably lie about the big ones, too. I don't know many liars, but the ones I do know have a way of making life pretty miserable for those around them, so if you'll excuse me, I'll be on my way."

Juggling the lamp, he dug into his back pocket and emerged with his wallet. "At least take your money—"

She waited as he opened the wallet and extracted a twenty. "It's all I have. Take it."

"I don't have change," she said briskly.

"Just keep the whole thing."

Gina had no desire to owe Alan Kincaid anything. As she opened her car door and slid behind the wheel, she said, "Keep your money." With that, she started the car and drove away, purposely not looking back.

2

"**I**s she gone?"

Alan closed the front door behind him and faced five-feet-one inches of walking insecurity—Sara, a slender girl with a dusting of freckles across her nose, decent enough grades and few friends. One thing she did have was the voice of an angel, and it was there, with the school choir, that she overcame her shyness. She was standing at the bottom of the stairs, a loose black jumper with dangling store tags obliterating what little figure she had.

"Yes, she's gone," he said.

Sara flashed a rare smile and held out her hands. Alan gave her the lamp, which she regarded with glowing eyes. "I can't believe you got it back," she whispered.

"Neither can I," he said with a sigh.

"Did the lady make you pay a lot for it?"

My pride, Alan thought, but that wasn't true. He was the one who had made up the keepsake story. "It doesn't matter," he said. "It's all yours now, Sara. This time hide it where Uncle Joe can't find it, okay?"

"Okay. Uncle Joe still doesn't know it was me who wanted the lamp, does he?"

"No. I promised you I wouldn't tell a soul, and believe me, I kept my promise."

"He just teases me all the time."

"I know, honey, but like I told you before, it's the way he shows affection."

Sara nodded, but her eyes remained unconvinced. Clasping the lamp in both hands, she said, "Thanks, Al. Now everything will be perfect—"

He said, "Sara," with the vague idea of cautioning her about pie-in-the-sky ideas, but by then, she'd turned and run up the stairs to her room. He hadn't even had a chance to chastise her for forgetting to warn him about the damn cookies!

Okay, so maybe he hadn't really done her any favors by getting the lamp back, but she'd been so despondent and he was used to trying to make things better for her. That's what a parent did for his kid, even if he wasn't really a parent.

For a second, he thought about the look of disappointment he'd discerned in Gina's eyes when Uncle Joe dropped his bomb, and his pleasure over returning the lamp to Sara waned. Perhaps he could have accomplished the same thing without the subterfuge, but he doubted it. Gina had said herself that it was the word "keepsake" that had attracted her. Besides, what did he care if this woman thought he was a jerk and didn't want anything else to do with him?

But he did care. For the first time in more years than he liked to think about, he did care. For a while, he'd been overwhelmed by the death of his stepmother and his father and the sudden and urgent need to move back into this house and become a parent for Sara and Rob. Then Uncle Joe had appeared at the door, broke as usual—he hadn't been lying about the old man's enchantment with the track—and Alan had had to figure out a way to incorporate him into this odd household. Add his contracting business to pay the bills and the sailboat he was building in the backyard so he had something to dream about, and it didn't leave a lot of time or energy for dating.

And then today, out of the blue, Gina Cox had walked into his kitchen, and from the first glimpse of her, he'd known she was different.

She was exquisite, too. Her wavy hair glistened, her huge eyes betrayed every emotion, her body was trim and athletic. Life was as busy now as it had been before she'd appeared, but suddenly he found himself pondering ways to fit a short fling with a beautiful coppery-headed woman into his plans. He was relieved she'd acted uninterested in the idea of marriage—he definitely didn't have enough time or energy for that kind of commitment. Then again, she'd also sounded sour about men in general; *that* could be a stumbling block.

Well, what the hell did it matter? She was furious with him, and he didn't need another complication in his life, anyway. With a silent curse, he went out through the front door, digging in his pocket for the keys to his truck, his mind focused on finding cookies for Sara's school, Gina nothing more than a bittersweet memory, a beautiful what-might-have-been.

Gina tapped her fingers on the arm of her chair and interrupted her caller. "I know you liked the idea of a brass lamp. So did I, but it's gone and that's that."

I should have demanded Alan give the lamp back to me! This thought had been coming and going over the past week, her anger with Alan Kincaid and his duplicity a slow burn that gave no indication of subsiding. Once she'd found out he had been lying to her, she should have run with the lamp. Maybe she should call him and insist— The thought died right there. She knew she'd never call.

Meanwhile, her restaurant client was threatening to pull his business.

"I have a new idea," she said, striving to make her voice sound tempting.

"It better be good," he said ominously.

"We change the name from Aladdin to The Flying Carpet. Instead of a lamp, we use Oriental carpets and Moroccan tapestries. We'll find a really gorgeous rug to suspend in the entry so it looks as though it's flying, as though it's waiting to whisk your guests off to magical places."

After a long pause, he sighed. Grudgingly, he said, "That's not bad. Can you make up a presentation to show my investors?"

"I'll have it by tomorrow," Gina assured him.

He hung up on her with a decisive click. Smiling, Gina put down the receiver. She'd dodged a bullet, all right. Moving out of the office she'd shared with Howard had wiped out her paltry savings account. Not that she begrudged spending the money—anything was preferable to being near Howard—but she couldn't afford to lose a lucrative account.

The relief was short-lived, for in the next second, she caught sight of the newspaper she'd bought at lunch so she could do her weekly check on local garage sales. The newspaper reminded her of Alan, whose face suddenly swam in front of her eyes. It had been doing that for days, appearing at odd moments, in the shower, on the toaster, in a clock face. He always looked the same—eyes snapping, a smile toying with his lips. She remembered his words, his "Trust me," and she wondered what he'd meant.

The ads were uninspired this week, and Gina found none to circle with her red pen before she came to the last box in the second column. *"Gina,"* it read. *"I'm sorry."*

She stared at the words for a minute or an hour, it was hard to tell. Again, Alan's face appeared—she had no doubt in her mind that it was his ad—and again, she stared into dark brown eyes that had seemed so honest at first. As if a person could tell what went on inside someone else's head just from his eyes! Howard, for instance, had the bluest eyes in the world, eyes that screamed innocence, eyes that hid duplicity. She'd learned the hard way that eyes weren't necessarily the window to a man's soul.

A hearty knock sounded on her door. As she'd been in the office only ten days, this was a rare-enough occurrence to make Gina furrow her brow. The only appointment she had was with Julia Ann Dunsberry and that wasn't for another thirty minutes. The woman wasn't known, to say the least, for her early arrivals.

The door opened as Gina stood; to her utter astonishment, Alan Kincaid walked in, pausing just inside the door. The visions Gina had been experiencing had seemed so real that for a second she wondered if she was seeing Alan's face superimposed on another man's body.

"Hello," he said, and it was Alan's voice.

She nodded curtly, both annoyed and pleased to see him. In worn jeans and boots, arms crossed, eyes wary, he seemed very out of place in her office. She saw him glance at the shelves of books, the table laden with carpet samples, the hanging rings of upholstery samples and the rack of brochures on everything from lighting to French provincial furniture, and the wary look increased.

Good. Served him right to feel uncomfortable.

Without moving any farther into the room, he asked, "May I speak to you for a moment?"

She wanted to tell him to get lost, but she realized the only way she was going to get this man's face off her toaster and out of her shower was to listen to what he had to say. "For a moment," she said.

He crossed to the swivel chair in front of Gina's desk. She watched him move and remembered the way he'd swept up the broken cookies. She was finding it very disconcerting to be so attracted to such a louse.

Her gaze followed his to the newspaper. "Did you see my apology?" he asked.

She nodded. "How did you find this office? I'm not in the phone book yet...."

"I went to your old office, the one that is listed. A guy with blond hair—I think his name was Howard—told me you'd moved out a couple of weeks ago. I told him I wanted to hire you to redecorate my house, so he gave me your new address."

Good old Howard. "So, do you want to hire me to redecorate your house?"

"No," he admitted.

"You lied," she stated flatly.

"Yes, but not in print this time. That apology is real, Gina."

For a few seconds, they regarded each other in silence. Gina decided her memory of his face hadn't done him justice. His dark brows were straight and luxurious, his eyes so brown they bordered on black. A straight nose, generous lips, assertive chin and square jaw completed the picture. He was wearing a long-sleeved blue shirt that looked heavenly on him. None of this changed who and what he was.

"Why are you here?" she asked bluntly.

"I felt bad about the other day—"

"Well, so did I. I don't like being manipulated."

"I gathered as much."

"But you've said you're sorry, so that's that. Apology accepted."

He leaned forward and gazed at her intently. At last he cleared his throat. "Just like that?"

"What's the point in being angry with a man I'll never see again?"

He nodded curtly, but made no move to leave.

Gina tapped a pencil against the newspaper. "What do you want, Alan? I've said I'll accept your apology." Standing, she added, "Now, if you don't mind, I'm expecting a client—"

"Actually," he said slowly, "I'm not here to apologize. I need you to do something for me."

The nerve of this guy! "So that's why you apologized, because you want a favor?"

"No. I placed the ad before I discovered I needed to talk to you again."

She sat back in her chair.

He reached into his breast pocket and withdrew a folded five-dollar bill, which he put on top of the newspaper. "I want you to take this money," he said. "It's what I owe you for the lamp."

They both stared at the folded bill. Gina finally said, "Okay, I'll take the money."

Haltingly, he added, "Gina, I know this is going to sound, well, crazy, but I need a bill of sale."

"Why?"

"For taxes," he said quickly.

For thirty seconds she stared at him, wondering if this was a joke. But he didn't flinch, he just returned her gaze until finally, Gina broke into laughter.

He appeared offended as she got up from her chair, still laughing, and went around the desk until she was standing in front of him. Perching on the edge of the desk, arms folded across her chest, she stared down at him as he looked up at her. This vantage point gave her a slight feeling of power, something she instinctively felt she needed.

"No," she said at last.

Now he looked startled. "Why not?"

"Because you're still lying to me."

A protest seemed to die on his lips. It was clear he didn't like her taking the upper hand, so to speak, because he stood, too, and faced her. They were very close. Gina couldn't help but notice the man; not only was he less than a foot away, but it seemed as though his very presence charged the air around her.

"You're right."

His admission startled her. "I'm right!"

"Yes, yes, you're right. I don't need the receipt for taxes. I need it to prove I own the lamp."

Tilting her head, Gina said, "Why am I beginning to think there are diamonds glued in the spout of that lamp?"

"I wish."

"Then if the lamp isn't valuable, why do you need to prove you own it?"

A steady stare was followed with a rush of words. "So I can give it to someone else and then they can own it. When you didn't take the money, you didn't relinquish ownership, so I wasn't free to give it to...someone else, and so now, it's not really theirs."

"Alan—"

"I know, I know," he said, throwing up his hands. Hitching them on his waist and casting a leveling glare that interrupted Gina's ability to breathe properly, he added, "I know this all sounds like something a child would come up with, but it's the truth. Believe me, if I were lying, it would sound better than this."

"I don't know," she said with a reluctant smile. "That tax thing was pretty thin."

"So, will you write me a receipt?"

She went back around the desk and sat down. "The only way I'll take this money and write you a bill of sale is if you tell me what the devil is going on."

He stared at her another long moment, then he, too, sat down. "I told Sara it would come to this. She gave me the okay to tell you the truth as a last resort."

"Trust me," Gina said with a humorless smile. "This is a last resort."

"I can see that. Okay, here goes. About a month

ago, Sara found the lamp in a pile of junk I'd cleared out of an old garage. She asked me if she could have it. I thought she wanted it to dress up her room or something—you know how thirteen-year-old girls are. I never dreamed the kid actually thought the thing was magical.''

Gina whispered, "Magical?"

"Yeah. Apparently she made a wish, and the very next day what she wished for came true. She wanted to join the choir, but she'd always lacked the nerve to even try out for it. Anyway, she made that wish, tried out and got in.''

"Does she have a good voice?"

"Yes.''

"So she really got into the choir because she finally tried out for it?''

"Of course. But she doesn't see it that way—she gives all the credit to that damn lamp.''

Gina smiled. "I would have believed in the lamp, too. When I was her age, I mean.''

"Well, it did work, in a way. It gave her the courage to reach out for something she wanted, which is why I keep indulging her on this thing. After she made the first wish, she hid the lamp in the garage. Uncle Joe found it, you bought it, and Sara came completely unglued. That's when she finally told me about her belief in its powers. She swore me to secrecy, begged me to get it back. I used the keepsake bit because I was hoping someone would take pity on me. I never meant to lie, not really.''

"What you mean," Gina interrupted, "is that you never meant to get caught.''

He looked chagrined. "I suppose, especially not by

someone like you. Anyway, after you left the other day, I gave the lamp back to Sara and she made her second wish. I gather it didn't come true. She's been quizzing me for days about what happened when you returned it. When she discovered you wouldn't accept payment, she decided that's why the lamp won't work. In her mind, you still own the lamp and so her wish can't come true.''

"What did she wish for this time?" Gina asked, caught up in this tale despite her determination not to be.

"I have no idea. She won't tell me."

Gina nodded. Even the smallest child knew magic secrets were to be made in privacy. She believed Alan's story because it all made sense—protecting a younger half sister was both admirable and rather touching. The fact remained, however, that Alan was quite comfortable with rearranging the truth when the situation called for it. She hated to be paranoid, but wasn't he just a more noble version of Howard?

"So, how about it?"

Gina had told Alan she was through with men. It was good she'd remembered this statement. He had a way of siderailing her convictions. She said, "I'll be happy to write out a receipt."

"Fantastic. I owe you one."

She smiled faintly as she rolled open the top drawer of her filing cabinet. "You don't owe me a thing," she said.

"Sure I do. Thanks to you, Sara will now feel she owns her lamp and make another wish. Hopefully, it will move her closer to maturity. Speaking of wishes, how about yours? That pesky client still annoying you?''

Gina closed the drawer and opened the bottom one, pausing for a second to reflect on his question. ''You know, it's odd, but this is the first week since I accepted her account that she hasn't called me three times a day with a dozen ludicrous ideas. Fact is, I haven't seen or heard from her since last Friday. But she's due here in a matter of minutes.''

''She sounds kind of interesting. Maybe I should hang around,'' Alan said.

''She's married,'' Gina commented as she dug through her files. ''On the other hand,'' she added as she finally found the receipt book, ''Julia Ann is about twenty years younger than her husband. I believe she's his fourth or fifth wife.''

''And your point is—''

''She's very attractive.''

''So obviously, I would want to check her out, is that what you're implying?''

''Let's just say Julia Ann is fond of spandex.''

''Which makes her attributes all the easier to see? Well, you know us men. Wrap a pretty woman up in rubber and we turn into animals.''

''Ah, sarcasm.''

''Well, really.''

''Isn't it true?''

''No, as a matter of fact, it isn't.''

''And I suppose you're the exception?''

''I'm one of them.''

''You don't care what a woman looks like?''

''And you don't care what a man looks like?'' he countered.

"No," she said, which she recognized immediately wasn't true. She'd done little else but review his looks since she'd met him, making her a world-class phony! Should she apologize? So far, that was all their relationship was based on, apologies. Wait, what relationship? He was just a guy with a mixed-up little sister. She wrote out a receipt for five dollars, mentioning Alan Kincaid by name, making sure it was clear and very complete.

Alan took it and they both got to their feet. "So," he said, "is everything square between us?"

It was hard not to respond to the sincere tone of his voice. "Yes."

"Which means we can start again?"

Gina folded her arms across her chest. "What do you mean?"

"I mean, I've explained like crazy and now I want to know if you'll have dinner with me tomorrow night."

She narrowed her eyes, ignoring the wild way her heart suddenly began thumping around. "I don't think—"

"It will give me an opportunity to repay you for your...kindness in this matter."

"I already told you—"

"I know what you told me, Gina. I'll be honest with you, I know it's a virtue you admire. I don't just want to thank you for tolerating Sara's teenage angst and my clumsy attempts at dealing with it. This is an invitation to have dinner with me. If that's not clear enough—I'm asking you out on a date. I know you've had your share of those."

"And how would you know what I've had my share of—"

"Because no woman could be as touchy about men as you are without prior experience."

"I'm not touchy," she insisted, but, of course, she was. She added, "We don't know each other."

"Well, that's kind of the point of dating," he said dryly.

"You said you didn't have the time or inclination for dating."

"I said I didn't have the time or inclination for marriage, which is a whole different story. Sara's choir is having a concert this weekend, and I'm going to the performance tonight. Rob and Uncle Joe are going tomorrow night, which means that Saturday, I'll have a rare night off. I'd like to spend it with you."

I'm through with men. She'd told him this, had he forgotten? Had she? She needed to make up an excuse, but her mind was empty.

"You're nursing a broken heart," he said.

"Absolutely not!"

"Wounded pride?"

She shrugged.

"It's just dinner," he said, leaning forward again, tapping her on the arm, smiling.

Face it, she told herself. *You're attracted to this guy. He wants to have dinner with you, which means the attraction must be mutual. But he doesn't have time for a relationship, and you're through with men, at least for a while. You simply shouldn't go through the ordeal of another Howard. On the other hand, this is just dinner. Maybe we'll be bored with each*

other by the time dessert is served, which means we
can both get back on track without speculating about
what might have been. She said, "Why not?" before
she could talk herself into saying no.

He didn't answer her with words. He didn't need
to. The look in his eyes reflected his pleasure. Gina
felt riddled with both anxiety and excitement.

Into this highly charged atmosphere came the loud
ringing of a phone, and they both jumped, startled.
Gina grabbed it after the first ring and turned her back
on Alan.

It took her some seconds to concentrate on what
was being said, so that as the speaker finished, she
had to ask him to repeat his message. She mumbled
a few words of condolence and promised to arrive the
following morning. When she turned back to Alan he
was looking at her with concern.

"Is something wrong?" he asked, taking a step toward her.

"You're not going to believe this," Gina said. "I
don't believe this."

"Believe what? Who was on the phone?"

"Cedric, the Dunsberry's social secretary. He informed me that Julia Ann just remembered her appointment with me. It's not the first time she's done
this, you understand, but this time she has a good
excuse—seems she tumbled down a flight of stairs
last Saturday morning. She broke her right ankle and
twisted her neck."

Alan's eyebrows shot up his forehead.

"Great, huh? Twelve hours after I wish the woman
would leave me alone, she falls down a flight of
stairs!"

Alan touched her hand. "What are you getting at?" he demanded.

"You know what I'm getting at," she whispered.

He tightened his grip. "Now, wait a second. This is a coincidence, nothing more. There are no such things as magic lamps."

"I know that," Gina snapped, but the irrational fear was growing in her stomach that it wasn't a coincidence at all. She suddenly felt nauseous.

"Gina, look at me. There is no genie in that lamp. It was a coincidence."

She looked up into his eyes. It came to her in a flash she was acting just like his little sister, assigning magic and hoodoo to a lifeless object. She withdrew her hand from his grasp.

"Did I understand correctly that you're going to see Julia Ann tomorrow?" he quizzed her.

"What—oh, yes. I'll take all the samples over there. In fact, from now on, I'll be dragging everything over there."

"It'll do you good to see her," he said with utter confidence. "It'll lay your mind at rest. You'll see, there will be a perfectly logical explanation for her fall."

"You don't understand," Gina said. "That house is full of subcontractors. There are two guys painting the entryway even as we speak, and another crew hanging wallpaper in the study. There's a carpenter in the servants' quarters who is rebuilding a closet and a whole group of them in the basement installing a bowling alley of all things. There are plumbers and men installing drywall...what if she tripped over one of them or their tools?"

"Do you carry insurance?"

"Of course."

"Well, then, if she sues you, your insurance rates will skyrocket."

"How comforting."

"There are worse things than losing a little money," he said.

"I know that!"

He smiled smugly. "Well, now, at least you're worried about *real* things and *real* people."

She regarded him with a frown. "I suppose you're now in your 'Let big brother chase away the demons and put a smile on your face' mode."

He had the grace to look embarrassed. "I suppose so. But Gina, I have no desire to be your big brother."

"Good. I don't need a big brother." She stood and tugged on the bottom of her jacket, literally as well as figuratively pulling herself together.

He glanced at his watch. "I guess I'd better go."

She nodded, still racked with conflicting emotions but on her way back to equilibrium.

"Where shall I pick you up?"

"Pick me up?"

"For our date."

Their conversation about a date seemed to Gina as though it had occurred a zillion years before, and it was on the tip of her tongue to call the whole thing off. Just then she met his gaze. There was something in his eyes that made her feel he was expecting her to back out, and this contrarily made her determined to see it through—but on her terms.

"Since I know where you live, I'll pick you up. Seven okay?"

He didn't look thrilled by her idea, but perhaps he heard the note of finality in her voice. He nodded. "Seven is fine."

They sealed the deal with a nod. The queasy feeling in Gina's stomach returned.

3

The Dunsberry mansion was nestled in five acres of prime real estate. A long circular drive led to a cobbled courtyard surrounded by iron railings and cement fountains. The house itself was made of brick with white shutters and trim. It truly was a splendidly designed house, proportioned well, built with great craftsmanship, maintained to perfection, and Gina felt a certain responsibility to uphold the same distinction inside as existed outside. This goal wasn't as easily accomplished as it sounded.

She parked behind a fleet of vans. As Charles Dunsberry had made it clear that cost was not as important as expediency, she had arranged for different subcontractors to work six days a week, so she wasn't surprised to find the painters and the paper hangers and the electricians and the carpenters here on a Saturday morning.

Gina opened the trunk and gathered an armload of sample books. It would take a few trips to get all this into the house, but for some reason she felt good about having to put herself out, kind of like doing penance. She felt guilty about Julia Ann's accident, that was the problem. Actually, she mused as she staggered under her load, the bigger problem was that she was silly enough to believe she had a reason to feel guilty!

The front door was ajar, so she was able to nudge it open with her shoulder and step into the huge tiled entry. Cedric, Julia Ann's secretary, immediately appeared in a doorway off to her left, pad of paper and pen in hand. Sparing her no more than a stiff nod, he walked briskly away from her.

Charles Dunsberry came through the open doorway next. As Gina walked beneath a long board of scaffolding supported by two ladders, he crossed the hall toward her. Charles was a middle-aged man with a clipped mustache and wire-framed glasses; his face was long and thin, his chin weak. Gina found herself comparing this pale man to Alan Kincaid—Charles came up wanting in every aspect. He had none of Alan's fire, none of his sparkle, none of his sensual good looks...and he held none of Alan's dangerous attraction!

"Terribly good of you to come," Charles said.

She said truthfully, "I was so sorry to hear about Julia Ann's fall—"

"Yes, yes. The poor dear is quite badly shaken."

"Oh—"

"Which is why I think we must shift our focus from the servants' wing to the solarium. Properly done, the room will become a sanctuary for Julia Ann."

The solarium, adjoined to the back of the house with wide double doors, had been abandoned for years. Plants were now dead or overgrown, walkways were cracked, windows leaked, plumbing and electricity were antiquated. Gina had been looking forward to reviving this room, but it had been agreed on from the first that it would be the last project undertaken.

"And we'll want it by the All Hallows' eve party, of course. Think how smashing an unveiling will be! A real coup for you, my dear—everyone who is anyone will be here."

"Seven weeks from now?" Gina squeaked.

"Is that a problem?"

Whoa, talk about a double-edged sword! This was her chance to shine or fall flat on her face. Shifting her load, Gina mentally reviewed who was working on what and how she could change things around.

"I know you can handle it," he said. "Meanwhile, my dear wife is talking about flamingos. *I trust you'll take care of this....*" He followed this statement with a curt nod and left, confident he didn't need to wait around for a reply.

She'd need more help, that was all there was to it. Tonight she'd start making calls. It was a busy time of year, however. Everyone wanted their homes jazzed up for the coming holidays, though most focused ahead to Thanksgiving and Christmas and not Halloween!

Gina paused at the doorway of the sitting room, the first room she'd done and her favorite, as it was a traditional blend of flame-stitch patterns, cherry tables and floral upholstery. The windows were high and generous, looking out on a bank of trees that Gina knew shielded the house from a view of the tennis court.

Julia Ann was seated in one of the chairs, propped

up by mounds of pillows. She was a southern belle, all right, but a nineties kind of southern belle. No hoop skirts for Julia Ann, just brief spandex tops and skin-tight nylon shorts. Mounds of apricot curls topped the effect like a frilly bow on a package. Attractive in an up-front kind of way, she looked so out of place in this classic mansion that Gina was startled anew each and every time she saw her.

The jolt was amplified today by the fluorescent pink cast on her lower right leg and a yellow neck brace.

Julia Ann's eyes fluttered open as Gina set the books on the butler's table in front of the sofa. "How y'all doing?" she drawled, adding without pause, "hand me that pillow, no, not that one, the little one. I swear, I ache all over. Where is that nurse?"

Gina glanced over her shoulder. "I don't know. Shall I go look—"

"Don't bother, she's probably lurking in the kitchen. The woman grazes her way through life. I suggested she use my exercise tapes—I mean, it's not as though I can use them—but she's too lazy. Put the pillow under my foot, Gina."

Amid much advice, Gina positioned the pillow, then perched on the edge of an armchair. Folding her hands between her knees and leaning forward, she said, "I was so sorry to hear about your accident."

"Charles thinks I was lucky not to break my neck."

Gina swallowed. "What happened?"

"That's the weird part—I don't have the slightest idea! One minute I was coming down the stairs between the third and the second floors, and the next thing I knew, I'm in the hospital.''

"You must have tripped—"

"In my slippers? Besides, y'all know those stairs. There isn't a thing to trip on!"

Gina leaned forward. "What were you doing on the third floor? There's nothing up there yet."

"That's the other odd part of this whole thing, because I don't ever go up there, not ever, but a few hours after you left here last Friday afternoon, I got to thinking about how you said we could remake the old nursery into a theater, and I thought to myself, Julia Ann, honey, y'all just have to go up there and see if it will work. Well, I did, and frankly, Gina, the place is gloomy! Maybe if we cut a window thing in the roof it would brighten things up."

"A skylight in a theater is certainly a different approach," Gina said diplomatically, but her thoughts were elsewhere: *Julia Ann went upstairs because of something I said...and the thought first occurred to her on Friday afternoon!*

"And now it will be weeks, maybe months, before I can help y'all around here. I can't climb stairs or nothing. I just have to sit here depending on our servants, and most of them have been with Charles for ages and just plain out don't like me!"

"I'm sure that's not true," Gina said politely.

"Ha! Take that prissy Cedric. Have you ever met a snootier man? I swear, I don't even have the energy to organize the Halloween bash, which leaves the whole thing in Cedric's hands. I know I can't trust him, he's a royal pain in the neck."

In the recent past, Gina's thought on that last re-

mark would have been along the lines of *Well, it takes
one to know one.* Now she smiled weakly as she realized Julia Ann was right—she wouldn't be "helping" for a while. The wish really had come true.

"What's wrong with you?" Julia Ann demanded.

"Nothing." Gina instantly reined in her wild
thoughts. Coincidence, that's what Alan had said, and
on this matter, he was absolutely right. The alterna-
tives were just too ridiculous to consider. She picked
up a sample book and opened it, thumbing through
the pages for pictures to show Julia Ann. "Let's talk
about the solarium," she said, striving for profession-
alism. "I hear you've been thinking about flamingos."

Julia Ann waved away the suggestion. "I can't
concentrate on decorating right now, Gina, my foot is
throbbing. You work on it. Just be sure to think pink!
Oh, gosh, I need more pain medication, I don't care
how long it's been." She produced a small bell from
beside her thigh and rang it. "Where is that blasted
nurse?" Wrinkling her forehead, she added, "I bet
you a sackful of pigs she's in the kitchen again!"

Alan stared at his younger brother, who was standing at the sink, wolfing down the second of two pas-
trami sandwiches. "Don't they ever feed you at the
dorms?"

Rob nodded as he poured himself a third glass of
milk. He was slightly shorter than Alan, with similar
coloring they'd both inherited from their mother.
"It's *what* they feed me," he said. "Brown stuff and
yellow stuff. Once in a while, I need real food." He
downed the milk and added, "What smells so good

in here? It's Italian food, right? When did you learn how to cook?''

Alan was purposely evasive. He didn't want to explain himself to Rob. Sure, he had food keeping warm in the oven—it was part of his master plan. If Gina thought he was going to meekly fold himself into her little car and drive to some stuffy restaurant where he couldn't even hold her hand, she was wrong. They'd eat here, giving him home-court advantage. He might be rusty in the romance department, but he wasn't completely without his tricks. He wanted to impress her, he wanted to lower her guard, he wanted to win her heart, he wanted to consume her—not necessarily in that order.

''Uncle Joe said you had a really hot date tonight,'' Rob said as he finished the last of the sandwich.

''I have a date, yes,'' Alan admitted.

Rob leaned against the counter, crossing his legs at the ankle. ''How long has it been since you went out?''

''Too long.''

''You want some advice from your younger and more experienced brother?''

As Alan put the milk back in the refrigerator, he glanced at his brother and said, ''No. Absolutely not.''

Rob put an arm around Alan's shoulder. ''Don't be too nice to her,'' he cautioned. ''Women like guys who don't care, it really turns them on.''

''I suppose I should slap her around a little?''

''You can joke if you want, Al, but this is choice advice I'm giving you here. Just ignore her. The more you really like her, the less you show it.''

"And this is the secret of your success?"

Rob nodded. "Try it."

Alan was saved coming up with a response by the emergence of Uncle Joe and Sara. The latter was dressed in a white blouse and her new jumper, the official uniform of the choir. She had her hair pulled back in a ponytail, a style that made her look nine years old. Her cheeks were flushed, and her eyes were so bright they were like burning stars in her face.

He put the back of his hand against her forehead. "Do you have a fever?"

"Bet she's got stage fright," Rob taunted, slapping Sara with a dish towel.

"Get your jacket, Rob, we're going to be late." This from Uncle Joe, who was pocketing the race form.

The two men disappeared down the hall. Alan and Sara followed them a few seconds later, walking side by side. "Are you sure you're okay?"

She stopped him midhall, glancing over her shoulder to make sure they were alone. "I made my wish again," she said so softly he had to strain to hear her.

"Oh—"

"So tonight it will come true," she added.

"Sara—"

"Hush! Uncle Joe and Rob don't know." And with that, she wheeled around and joined the others, Alan looking after her. He'd hoped she'd become discouraged with wishing by now, but it seemed the opposite was true. A gut feeling told him he was going to regret ever getting that lamp back.

Despite her intention to treat this dinner as a meal and nothing else, Gina dressed with care. She had no idea what kind of restaurant Alan would decide upon, so she chose a floral skirt, creamy silk blouse and a coordinating vest. The blouse had been a gift from Howard. As she stood in front of Alan's door, she wished she hadn't worn it; she didn't want to be reminded of Howard in any way, shape or form, not tonight. The thought crossed her mind to run home and change clothes, but just then the door opened and she was face-to-face with Alan. Wait, not Alan—a dead ringer, though, except that this man was younger and slightly shorter.

"You've got to be Al's date," he said with a smooth smile. "But whoa, how did someone like my brother wind up with someone like you?"

Gina, speechless, finally saw Joe and Sara, and behind them, Alan, who was covering his eyes with his hand, massaging his temples. His muffled voice could be heard saying, "My brother is just leaving."

Rob gave a broad thumbs-up gesture.

"It was nice to meet you," Gina said, and, glancing down at Sara, added, "I hear you're singing tonight. Good luck."

"Thanks," Sara chirped, and then they were all moving past her, chattering, on their way to the car that was parked at the curb. All except Alan, who stood facing her alone now, his hand back at his side, his brow furrowed as he stared after his family.

He was wearing black slacks and a black turtleneck, the single color making him look even taller than he was. With his coloring, the result was striking. Each time Gina saw this man he seemed slightly different. Tonight, gone was the charming flirt, gone the contrite older brother. Instead, she found a delectable man with a brooding expression that exuded sexiness...pure, unadulterated sexiness.

All day long she'd been uneasy, and she'd blamed it on the disquieting talk she'd had with Julia Ann. Now she was wondering if it had more to do with Alan than magic lamps, because the feeling was growing more intense instead of less. For a woman determined not to get sucked into another meaningless relationship, she realized she was standing right smack in the path of an approaching tornado. Where was a nice, safe root cellar when you needed one?

"Is something wrong?"

"I was about to ask you the same thing," she said.

He stared at her for a long count of ten before shaking his head. With the gesture, it seemed his mood lightened, as though he'd put whatever was bothering him on a mental back burner. The vitality that glittered in his eyes as he gazed down at her made Gina's breath catch.

He said, "Nothing is wrong, everything is damn near perfect. You look sensational. Come on in."

"I can wait outside," she said.

"Slight change of plans, hope you don't mind, but I thought we'd eat dinner here."

Gina hadn't expected this. "I thought we were going out."

"Are you afraid I might bite?" he asked playfully.

"I wouldn't put it past you," she said, sparing him a quick smile.

"Never, never on a first date."

"I'll remember that. It'll help me make a decision should the subject of a second date arise."

He laughed. "Last Christmas a client gave me a

gift certificate. I've had it in my wallet for ten months now—in fact, it expires this December. Anyway, the gift certificate is for her catering service. I called her yesterday after you agreed to dine with me, and exactly one hour ago, she delivered our dinner, which is in the oven bubbling away. Now, will you come in?''

She didn't want to. No, that wasn't honest. She wanted to very much, which was even worse. He was waiting for her to stop acting like a little kid. It wasn't as though she'd never been alone in his house with him before, so what was so different about tonight? Nothing, she admonished herself. Besides, right before she'd left the Dunsberry estate, she'd discovered the plumbers and the electricians had previous commitments that would make it impossible for them to get the solarium done in time. She wasn't sure what she was going to do about the plumbers, but the electrician was standing right in front of her...if he had the time and the inclination and she had the nerve to ask.

He closed the door behind her and led the way toward the kitchen. They passed a dining room table stacked with books instead of plates.

"It sure smells good," Gina said as they emerged into the kitchen. The table in here was cluttered with newspapers. Obviously, the caterer hadn't taken care of table setting. That was okay, Gina would offer to do it and thereby occupy herself as she coped with a major case of dating nerves.

"Alison, she's the caterer, made us her speciality, eggplant parmesan," he said. He opened the refrigerator and took out a huge salad bowl filled to the brim with mixed greens. He set the bowl on a tray that was already holding a bottle of red wine, two stemmed glasses, a carafe of dressing, silverware, napkins and salad plates. "I thought we'd eat outside. Would you mind opening the back door?"

Gina held the door ajar as he carried the tray out into the yard. She followed, pausing at the top of the steps at the sight that greeted her.

A half-finished sailboat took up most of the free space. On the decks and the cabin top, and twinkling through the ribs in the hull, were clusters of white candles burning brightly in the still air. At one end of the boat, Alan had set up a sprinkler—a determined spray of water washed over the bow, as though to remind the uninitiated that this was an oceangoing vessel, or would be one day. The stern was completely open. As she watched, Alan set the tray on a small table tucked into this tight space.

"This is beautiful," Gina said. In truth, it was more than beautiful, it was magical. "Did the caterer—"

"No way," he interrupted. "The candles were my idea. Do you like them?"

"Very much," she said. She was stunned with the time this effort must have involved. For a man who had mentioned more than once how little of that commodity he had, he'd sure gone out of his way to impress and enchant her. So...and here she acknowledged her suspicious nature...what was his angle?

He flashed her a dazzling smile from over his shoulder as he fumbled with a tape recorder. It came on with a bang and he turned it down.

Gina listened for a few seconds. "Seagulls?"

Pouring the wine, he agreed. "And ocean waves."

"I hear them. I have to warn you, I get seasick."

"I promise we'll never leave port," he said, handing her a glass of ruby red wine. Clinking his glass against hers, he added, "Here's to you, Gina Cox."

They wouldn't have to leave port for her to feel seasick, Gina thought to herself. Loss of equilibrium, insides twisted into tight knots—nerves, she decided. Plain simple nerves brought on not by rolling waves but by Alan Kincaid. Aware he was staring at her, and afraid of what he might see in her face if he looked at her closely, she strode purposefully toward the bow. "Are you building this boat all by yourself?"

"Yep. She's my thirty-foot escape. Not literally, not at the rate I'm going. But when I come out here and pound nails or fit boards, I can put the rest of my life behind me for a while."

Gina turned, intrigued by his comment. She hadn't known he was as close as he was, and they ended up almost nose to nose, so close she could actually feel his body heat, which perversely made her shiver. Taking a generous step backward, she said, "Why do you need to escape your life? If you don't like it, can't you change it?"

"You're cold," he stated flatly.

Was that it? Was that why she felt so tingly? She shrugged. "I thought we were going out to a restaurant, I didn't dress for the out-of-doors." Anxious to get the topic of discussion away from her shivering, which she suspected had little to do with the outside temperature, she added, "You didn't answer me."

"You mean about escaping? There's not much to say. My life is hectic, that's all. I'm a male twenty-nine-year-old mother to a thirteen-year-old girl, and that isn't going to change for a long time. It's bound to have its stressful moments and this damn lamp thing isn't helping.''

That was another thing Gina had told herself she wasn't going to do tonight: discuss a magic lamp with a fully grown man. She made herself stay silent, even though she was dying to ask about Sara's second wish. As she watched, Alan's expression, which had grown temporarily troubled, cleared again. Leaning against the trunk of a tree, folding his arms across his chest, he said, "Let's talk about you."

"Me," Gina said, racking her brain for a witty retort and coming up empty. This whole evening was entirely too personal, that was the problem. She'd expected a short ride in the car, a crowded restaurant, seats across a wide table, noise. What Alan had provided was the exact opposite.

"You. For instance, has anyone ever told you candlelight becomes you? You don't need to answer, surely by now some male admirer has taken care of this compliment. When I was lighting these candles, I imagined how you'd look. I was right."

Gina lowered her eyes because the intensity of Alan's gaze was about to ignite her. A fleeting thought of Howard scampered across her mind—he'd never made her feel this way, even at the first when she'd mistaken infatuation for love. Nerves? Sure, but not this heart-thumping anxiety.

"You're cold," he said again. Pushing himself away from the tree, he added, "I'll get you a sweater."

As he strode across the lawn toward the back door,

she fanned her cheeks with an open hand. She wasn't cold, she was on fire!

Common sense said that sitting in the dark, wearing his clothes, drinking his wine while seagulls cawed in the background was an absurd way to maintain distance, but common sense be damned, she wanted to. The sensuous curve of his lips, the half-lit planes of his face, the boat he'd crafted with his own hands and heart, even the sound of water spattering against wood—everything was so romantic.

Anyway, it was too soon to think in terms of an unlikely distant future. She'd done that with Howard and look what had come of it. She could handle Alan Kincaid—he was a charmer, all right, and a flirt. He had a knack of saying the right thing at the right moment, and whether or not it was sincere—well, that was open to discussion. All she had to do was remember these facts and everything would be fine. She took a second gulp of wine and fanned her face a little harder.

They ate dinner encased in the boat, seated on over-turned wooden crates padded with chair cushions. Alan wasn't sure what the food tasted like—the sight of Gina in his cranberry wool sweater was a feast for the eyes, which tempered his appetite. Her hair was curlier than it had been on the two previous times he'd seen her, and it framed her face, disrupting his equilibrium.

"This is very good," Gina told him. They'd moved past the salad and the eggplant, the garlic bread and the wine and were now nibbling on raspberry cheesecake. Alan had made a fresh pot of coffee—it was the one cooking chore in which he excelled.

"I'll pass your compliments on to Alison."

She nodded absently. All through dinner, he'd had the feeling she was biting her tongue, one moment on the verge of asking him something, the next, shying away. When she finally blurted out her question, it took him by surprise.

"Did Sara make her second wish?"

The surprise turned to amusement, but he didn't let it show. As Sara had accepted Gina into the Magic Lamp Loop, as Alan was beginning to think of it, he could answer without reservation. "Yes. Don't ask me what it is because she still hasn't told me." For a second, he was reminded of Sara's bright eyes and her utter confidence in the magic of the lamp and his equally strong conviction that ultimately she'd wish for something that couldn't possibly come true by chance or happenstance. He glanced at his watch. She would be home in less than an hour.

"I wouldn't say my wishes out loud, either," Gina mused, making another comment that startled him. "If I was a kid, I mean, and believed in such things as magic lamps."

He smiled at her serious expression. "I don't know, you made your first wish in front of me and it came true."

"Now you're teasing me."

"Just a little. And how is Julia Ann Dunsberry?"

"As outrageous as always. I'm redoing her solarium, and get this, she wants me to think pink."

"Which means?"

"Flamingos."

He laughed. "Will you give them to her?"

"I don't know."

He heaved a contented sigh as he set aside his fork. He'd have to run five miles in the morning instead of his customary three to work off tonight, he thought, but it had been worth it. He said, "At least she sounds like a real character."

"She is. Which reminds me, I'm going to have to move some of my contractors around to get his solarium done in time. Would you be interested in making an estimate on the wiring?"

Grinning, he said, "You're not afraid the sight of Julia Ann Dunsberry all done up in spandex will send me over the top?"

"I'm willing to take a chance," she told him.

"Then I'm your guy."

"It means a lot of work between now and Halloween. Will your schedule accommodate this?"

"Sure," he said with more confidence than he felt. Truth of the matter was he wasn't sure where he'd get the time for another job, especially one that needed to be completed by the end of October. There was the apartment complex he was presently working on, and after that a new clinic.... On the other hand, how could he say no to Gina Cox? After all, her offer had to mean she was as interested in seeing more of him as he was in seeing more of her. *Or maybe,* his cautious side whispered, *she just needs an electrician.* He added, "Did you discover how she managed to fall down her steps?"

"Apparently, she tripped on thin air."

"Is she the type who could trip on thin air?"

"I believe she is," Gina said with a sudden smile

that ignited her eyes and subsequently did funny little things to his insides.

For a few minutes they stared at each other. Alan wasn't sure what she was thinking, but he knew what he was consumed with—lust! The only question was how to go about the seducing of Gina Cox. Should he try Rob's approach, should he ignore her? Wait a second...Rob was nineteen years old. Alan was *not* going to start taking romantic advice from a kid!

"You're staring at me," she said softly.

"You're hard not to stare at."

She dropped her gaze.

Alan continued. "Uncle Joe remembers you came to the yard sale with a man. Mind if I ask who he is?"

"Not at all. His name is Howard Raskeller. At the time, he was my boyfriend."

"He's not your boyfriend now?"

"No."

He kept his voice mellow. "So, there's room for someone new? Or were you serious? Are you really through with men?"

After a lengthy hesitation, she cracked a quick smile and said, "Probably not forever."

"You sound unsure," he told her. Curiosity gnawed away at him. Who had broken up with whom? Was this Howard guy the man he'd met the day before when he went searching for Gina at her old office? If so, there might be trouble—the man was good-looking in a California beach kind of way and he had the same occupation as Gina—obviously, they shared common interests.

Tilting her head, she said, "Do I? I guess it's just

that men are so...well, hard to trust." She seemed to recall that she was currently addressing a man, for she immediately flashed him an apologetic smile. "What about you?" she asked.

Alan shrugged. "I date occasionally, but it seems to me most women are hell-bent on marriage."

"And you're not."

She stated it as a fact, she didn't ask. Obviously, he'd made his viewpoint clear on this matter. For a second he was tempted to answer in a way that would leave future doors open, but he realized almost immediately he couldn't do that. He liked Gina; he had no desire to lie to her or to misrepresent himself. He shook his head and said, "No."

His answer didn't seem to faze her one way or the other. He narrowed his eyes. "Why are you so bitter about men?"

"I have my reasons," she said evasively.

"Share them."

"I wouldn't want to bore you—"

"Trust me, you won't bore me."

"How do you know?"

"I just do."

Gina put down her coffee mug and stood. She squeezed past the table, standing at last on the grass, half in shadows. Glad for an excuse to stretch his legs, Alan followed her.

She was peering up into the night sky, past the branches of the trees, her gaze focused on the full September moon. Alan yearned to touch her, to put an arm around her shoulders, to... Instead, to keep his hands busy, he plucked a twig adorned with three or four leaves and spun it between his fingers. "Come on," he coaxed, "you know so much about my family. It's your turn." She brought her gaze to his face. Now the desire to hold her was expanding into the desire to ravish her.

"I'll tell you the abbreviated version," she said.

"Fair enough."

"It's fairly maudlin, so you'd better grab a hankie."

"I'll take my chances."

"It's up to you. We'll start with untrustworthy man number one: my father. He and my mother were not married when I was conceived. He ran off, and my mother turned to her parents for help. Grandfather is man number two. I admit he is ultimately trustworthy, but he's just as assuredly self-serving. Anyway, he made my mom a deal she couldn't refuse—she'd have the baby and then disappear for good and he and Grandmother would raise it. *Raise me.* Otherwise, I gather, she was on her own. My mother agreed to his terms, so I've never met either of my parents."

Alan stared at her face. All he could find there was a calm acceptance of what was to him an astounding situation. He wasn't sure what to say.

She continued. "My grandfather, as you might have already figured out, is a domineering autocrat who insists everything be done his way. My grandmother is just about as bad. Mother, apparently, was the weak link—she gave in to them both. Look what she gave up out of fear."

"You," he said softly.

"Don't get me wrong, I don't spend my life regretting what I've never had. My grandparents love me in their own way, and they did what they thought was best. Still, I can't help but wonder about my mother and how different life would have been for all of us if my father had accepted his responsibilities and stayed by her side."

Alan once again noticed Gina touching her locket. When she saw him watching her, she dropped her hand. "Man number three was twelve years old. I was eleven and a half when he kissed me in the back seat of an old bus that was transporting us both to camp. True to form, he then ignored me for the rest of the summer. Numbers four to twelve were various guys I met in high school and college. Some were great, some were creeps, none of them were major factors in my life. And then came Howard Raskeller."

"Untrustworthy man number thirteen," Alan said.

"You got it. Isn't thirteen a bad-luck number or is it only when it falls on a Friday? Come to think of it, I met Howard on a Friday. Anyway, Howard and I dated each other for the better part of two years, just long enough to begin talking about marriage. A few weeks ago, I happened to overhear one of our female clients tell her friend that she and Howard were jumping into bed every chance they got. I didn't believe her. I knew Howard, or I thought I did, and I was certain he wouldn't cheat on me. Still, her declaration led me to notice little things, like his not being where he said he was going to be and unexplained additions to his expense account. My suspicions were turning me into a snoop, which I hated. I waited as long as I could—until the night of the yard sale, actually—and then I confronted him. I wanted him to explain things. I wanted him to assure me I had it all wrong."

"But he didn't."

Gina laughed. "You can say that again. He sheepishly admitted having an affair not only with her, but another client, as well. Here I was saving myself for Mr. Right and he was spreading himself around like a tub of soft margarine!"

"So you broke up with him," Alan said, inordinately pleased.

"You bet your life I did."

"And moved out of your office."

"We shared the office. I left because I couldn't stand the thought of seeing that jerk every day. We divided up our clients and the furniture and that was that."

"And you haven't seen him since?"

"Nope."

"Don't you miss him?"

She gave him a long look and finally said, "No. That's odd, isn't it? You'd think I would be mourning a lost relationship."

Tossing the twig aside, he said, "Maybe you are."

She seemed to consider his words. This was one of the things he enjoyed about her—she spoke with thoughtfulness, not just to hear the sound of her voice.

"No," she said at last. "I can honestly say I don't miss Howard Raskeller one tiny bit. Except for next weekend…"

Her voice trailed off, leaving Alan curious. Again, he heard Rob cautioning him about showing too much interest and again he shrugged off the advice. "Why's that?"

"I have Sunday dinner with my grandparents once a month, kind of a duty call on all our parts, I think.

Last month, I finally told them about Howard and promised I'd bring him with me next time. For twenty-two Sundays, I'd steered away from even mentioning him, and five days after I do, I find out what a two-timing scoundrel he is. Dinner is a week from tomorrow, and lo and behold, no Howard. Grandfather will revel in my gullibility.''

Alan heard himself say, "I'll go. I'll buy a blond wig and pose as Howard."

"I'm afraid I waxed poetic about his blue eyes," she said with a smile.

"Dark glasses."

"You're a couple of inches taller—"

"I'll stoop."

"He has a cleft in his chin."

"I'll grow a beard."

Gina's smile changed character as she stared at him. It went from amused to something else, something so tantalizing he was moved to grasp her shoulders. She trembled beneath his hands, but she didn't draw away, nor did she lower her eyes. He took these as positive signs.

"You're very determined, and very, very beautiful," he said softly. She was, too. The moonlight bathed her face, softening her already exquisite features. She looked mysterious and desirable and somehow unattainable, and he wondered what she would do if he kissed her.

Well, what better way to find out than to do it? Slowly, deliberately, he lowered his head until their lips met. Hers were unbelievably soft and unexpectedly yielding. For some reason he thought she would be restrained. The lustiness he sensed in her response surprised and delighted him.

The second kiss quickly evolved, as the nebulous ache he'd felt since first meeting her crystalized into a surge of desire he was powerless to control. He pulled her close to him and completely lost track of who he was. All that existed was the woman he was kissing, the taste and smell of her, the feel of her body against his, the heady wonder of it all.

He got so wrapped up in the proceedings that it took him a second to realize she wanted to pull away. Reluctantly, he loosened his arms, keeping her in the circle of his embrace. Her expression did not reflect his joy, however, and he felt the euphoria of a moment ago begin to fade.

"I think I'd better go," she said as she exerted the smallest amount of pressure on his arms. He released her at once, a little confused, a lot disappointed.

"Gina?"

She'd turned away, but when he spoke her name, she paused. Her face was all but hidden in the shadow of an elm tree, but the deep glints that caught the light told him she was staring at him. Staring at him hard. Her voice shaky, she mumbled, "It's late...I have work tomorrow."

"On Sunday?" he asked her, unsure why her voice sounded so strange. Was it fear he detected? How could it be? It came to him in a flash that maybe he was coming on too strong, moving too fast, scaring the daylights out of her. His suspicions were confirmed when he took a step toward her and she backed into the tree.

"I have to design the solarium—we have to start work," she mumbled.

"But—"

"I'll leave your sweater inside...."

"You can give it to me later," he said.

"No, no," she insisted as she sidestepped him and the tree and began moving toward the house. "You'll...need your sweater."

The horrible thought occurred to Alan that maybe Rob was right! He didn't have time to plot strategy. He stopped following her, which seemed to slow her retreat. She faced him again. "Alan," she began, then paused, obviously searching for words.

As he wasn't at all sure he wanted to hear what she had to say, he jumped in with words of his own. "It was only a kiss," he said, attempting to sound urbane and sophisticated. "Nothing to get hot and bothered about."

Even with the poor lighting, he could tell she blushed. "I'm not—"

"You're running away."

"No—"

"Sure you are. I'd hate to think it was because of a meaningless kiss."

This earned him a startled glance. "Meaningless?"

"Don't get me wrong, it was very nice, but I bet you kissed numbers three to twelve without giving it a second thought."

She just stared at him.

He raised both hands in a nonchalant gesture. "No big deal, right? A beautiful fall night, wine and candles, a man and a woman—"

"And a meaningless kiss," she added, her voice icy.

He began to regret taking this tack.

She nodded as though some thought in her head had just clicked into place. "I should have known—"

"Ah, Gina—"

"You're right, of course."

As the door slammed behind her, Alan decided he was going to kill Rob....

4

Gina tore off the sweater and deposited it in a heap on the bathroom counter. Alan had followed her into the house, which had driven her into the bathroom where she could rearrange herself in private. As she tucked her blouse back into her skirt and buttoned her vest, she realized she was as angry with herself as she was with him. He'd made his agenda clear from the onset—a little charm, a little wit, a few stolen kisses, maybe a quick roll in the hay. It was she who had confused seduction with romance!

He said the kiss was meaningless. His words incited shame in Gina's heart because, for her, the touch of his lips on hers had been ambrosia. For a while there, she'd lost all the feeling in her hands and feet, her heart had stopped pumping, her lungs had stopped expanding, all functions had seemed to cease. And then, with a punch worthy of a karate master, all systems had kicked into overload.

That's why she had drawn away—she'd desperately needed to plant her feet again—things were progressing too quickly. She'd come here telling herself she could control him; what she hadn't bargained for was the need to control herself!

He'd chided her for overreacting, for taking a mere kiss seriously. He'd made her feel a fool again, curse him!

He was waiting for her by the front door.

"Now, Gina—" he said.

She cut him off. Not willing to let him know how deeply his comments had cut her, she flashed him a dazzling smile. "Dinner was delicious," she said brightly as she opened the door. She was rewarded with a confused blinking of his eyes. She added, "Thanks for everything."

They both turned as a car pulled up in front of the house. "What perfect timing, your family is home," she cooed.

The car's interior lights blinked on as the passenger door swung open. Sara tumbled from the vehicle and ran up the front path, her pale hair streaming out behind her, her hand over her mouth.

She flew through the door and tore up the stairs, Gina and Alan staring after her in openmouthed wonder.

They both jumped at the sound of Rob's voice. "That kid is getting to be a real space cadet," he groaned.

"What happened?" Alan snapped.

Uncle Joe ambled up the walk. "Don't ask us what's wrong with the girl. I thought the concert went pretty well. She didn't flub up or anything, did she, Rob?"

He shrugged. "I don't think so. She looked happy enough until we went to pick her up at the back door and she was in a panic. She cried all the way home. You've got to talk to her, Al."

Nodding, Alan lowered his gaze to meet Gina's and added, "Will you wait for me?"

"It's very late," she said, faking a yawn. She knew it was only a little after nine o'clock—what did she care if they all thought she went to bed with the sun? She was just glad to have an excuse to avoid any more private, and humiliating, conversations with Alan. "You'd better go see to Sara."

"I'll walk you to your car," Rob said as Alan looked from Gina toward the top of the stairs.

"What a great idea," she said.

Alan looked anything but pleased, but duty called, and with a resigned sigh, he started up the stairs. As Uncle Joe closed the front door behind them, Rob ushered Gina down the front path.

He cleared his throat as she paused to dig in her purse for the car keys. "Your name is Gina, right? Listen, do you mind if I ask how it went?"

"What?"

"Your date with my brother."

She walked around the car to the driver's door as she sought a reasonable way to answer him, but it seemed her hesitation spoke more clearly than any words might have done.

"That bad," Rob said, shaking his head.

"No...dinner was delicious, and the backyard was lovely—"

"It's not so good when a woman talks about that kind of stuff," Rob said seriously. He was standing on the sidewalk. He leaned over the top of the car, his arms extended and, with open hands, thumped the metal like a drum. Staring intently at Gina as she unlocked the door, he added, "Shoot, I gave him advice. I guess he didn't listen to me. What a hard-head.''

"You gave Alan advice?"

"Good advice, too, really choice stuff. Listen, you have to understand something about Al. The guy used to be a raging stud, he had them lined up out the door. I don't know what happened to him.''

"Maybe the responsibilities of raising Sara," Gina volunteered. She didn't add, *and you.*

He thumped on the car again. "Yeah. But, hey, so he's a little slow, so what? You've got to give him another chance.''

It took a lot of willpower not to straighten Rob out. In her estimation, his brother wasn't slow in any way, shape or form. However, she wasn't about to discuss Alan with Rob, so she kept her mouth clamped shut and smiled noncommittally.

She was just about to get into her car when the front door of the house opened and Alan appeared framed in the light. He dashed down the path, and despite Gina's determination not to fall under his spell again, she found her heart racing. If he begged her to stay, if he pleaded with her to hear him out, what would she do?

"I'm glad you haven't left yet," he said.

She warned herself about appearing too anxious. "I was just—"

"It's Sara," he added. "She wants to talk to you.''

This was not, to say the least, what Gina had expected. "She wants to talk with me? Why?"

He cast Rob a quick glance, which told Gina all she needed to know. Sara wanted to talk about the lamp, but Alan couldn't say so in front of Rob. Gina said, "I can't see how I could possibly help her."

"She asked for you specifically."

Gina met Alan's stare. She was utterly confused, not only by Alan and Sara and Rob, but also by her own tumultuous emotions.

"Will you come?"

"Yes. Of course," she said, only vaguely aware of Rob's curious expression as she followed Alan back up the path.

Sara's room was lit by a small electric lamp, the shade of which was covered with frolicking lambs. As the wallpaper was plastered with storybook characters and the windows draped with violet gingham, it was obvious to Gina the room had originally been decorated for a child, one who was now quickly turning into a young woman.

Gina sat on the edge of the bed next to Sara, whose golden head was bowed. The girl was folding and refolding the hem of her skirt, pressing the material against bony knees, hands shaking, breathing audible. Her straight, baby-fine hair fell forward, shielding Sara's profile from Gina's inquisitive gaze.

Now what?

The child was obviously upset. Gina's heart ached for her misery, but she was completely adrift as to how to proceed. Obviously, the second wish hadn't come true and the girl was having to face reality. While Gina was sorry it had all crashed down on Sara's head with such a resounding thud, she couldn't help but be relieved, too—after all, this went to prove what intellectually she had known all along: the brass lamp was nothing but a brass lamp. Period.

Biting her lip, she finally said, "Do you want to talk about it, Sara?"

Sara shook her head, and then she nodded.

Gina clasped her own hands together and waited.

The explanation, when it finally came, was stilted, the pauses long and deep. "I...I wished, you know, on the...lamp. I wished...for a boy...for Jason...to talk to me. Just a word or two."

"I see." Of course it was a boy, what else at thirteen? Gina sought words of either counsel or comfort, she suspected it didn't much matter which. Haltingly, she finally managed to say, "Ah, Sara, honey, haven't you kind of...suspected, deep in your heart, I mean, that the lamp wasn't really...well, magical?"

This comment was met with a quick intake of breath on Sara's part. The young girl shook her head violently.

Gina was left with a dilemma. Should she continue along this line and really kill Sara's dreams, or back down and thereby foster false hope?

"You don't understand," Sara said before Gina could make up her mind which tack to take. "He *did* talk to me!"

Now Gina was stunned. "What!"

Hesitation gone, sentences running together, she gushed, "Everyone knows Jason likes Amber, and she was there and she sat next to him and everything, but he ignored her and talked to me. He even asked me to a party. He's never even looked at me before."

Gina's first thought was that Sara's second wish had come true! Acknowledging this revelation as immaterial, she pushed it aside and took Sara's hands into her own. Sara finally met her gaze. Gina said, "But that's wonderful, isn't it?"

Sara shook her head again, but this time slowly. Her blue eyes dominated her face. "I didn't know what to say to him. I was scared. I sat there like a big dummy."

"Oh, I don't think—"

"I couldn't even tell him I wanted to go to the party with him. It was awful, and it's all because of the lamp!"

She pulled her hands from Gina's loose grip, dropped to her knees, retrieved a box from beneath the bed and tore off the lid. They both looked down at the brass lamp within the box.

"Amber Sinclair is really pretty and she's really popular and everyone knows Jason likes her a lot. But he talked to me because I wished that he would." She picked the lamp up and stared at it.

Gina, throwing caution to the wind, said, "Sara, really, this little brass lamp is just a little brass lamp. You've seen inside, you know there's no genie in there. Jason talked to you because you're an interesting, pretty girl, that's all."

For some moments, Sara held the lamp against her chest, and then, straightening her shoulders, she held it out to Gina. "You take it," she said softly.

"Me?"

The child stood. "Please. Just take it home with you so I can't make any more wishes right now. I don't…want it here. It's too weird."

Gina finally understood that Sara was frightened of the supposed powers of the lamp. She took it reluctantly, not only because she was unsure that Sara really wanted her to take the darn thing, but because by doing so, she was becoming even more deeply drawn into the circle of Alan's life. She said, "I'll keep it for you, how's that? Whenever you want it back, all you have to do is ask."

Relief brought a spot of color to each of Sara's pale cheeks. Obviously, she was grappling with conflicting feelings about the lamp and perhaps even with the process of growing up.

"You have to pay me," she said.

"My purse is downstairs," Gina told her. Sara looked as though she wanted this transaction completed immediately, so Gina dug in her pocket, withdrew a nickel and a wrapped hard candy and held them toward Sara on the palm of her hand. "This is all I have on me."

Sara took the offering. "It's fine."

"You're sure?"

She nodded, looking anything but sure.

"This is a new twist," Alan said. They were standing on the porch, alone. Gina had told him what transpired because it was in Sara's best interest for her guardian to know what a giant step she'd taken. All Gina really wanted now was to get away before he turned the conversation to a more personal topic.

"Yes. Well, I'd best be going—"

"Thank you," he said, interrupting her.

She carefully moved toward the steps. "For what?"

"For helping my crazy little sister."

For some reason, she was annoyed he'd referred to

Sara as crazy. Intellectually, she knew he said it in a kind of endearing way, so her protective reaction was the thing that was really crazy. Still, she leveled him with a stare. "Your little sister is going to be a woman before you know it."

He looked startled. "Sara?"

"Sure. She's right on the edge. You really should help her redecorate her room. Maybe a project like that would take her mind off magic lamps."

"That's the other thing I want to thank you for, taking that damn lamp out of this house. Maybe now things will return to normal."

"Hey, you're the one who advertised for its return," Gina snapped.

"Wait a second, I didn't mean—"

"It's not as though I foisted the thing onto you, you know. You're the one who advertised, you're the one who lied."

"Not *that* again," he moaned.

"I was perfectly happy using it for the restaurant."

"Well, now you have it back, do with it what you will."

She ignored the sarcasm in his voice. "It's too late, I've already submitted a new proposal, which the owner seems to like even better than the lamp."

"Then, despite the trouble my family has caused you, it's all worked out okay."

Gina nodded. The lamp was buried deep in the big black purse that was slung over her shoulder. She could feel it there. It was a reminder of Sara's fears and her own lapse into fantasy, and like it or not, it would forever remind her of Alan. She couldn't even throw it away because she had the distinct feeling Sara would want it back.

"About earlier—" he began, but she cut him off.

"Don't."

"I'd like to explain."

"Just...don't."

He frowned at her. Gina was glad to escape.

As her taillights rounded the corner, Alan swore softly to himself. He'd sure made a mess of this night. Getting a new love affair off the ground was always a tricky proposition, but he'd made things even worse by going on and on about meaningless kisses. Which reminded him, he owed Rob one. Little brother was lucky he'd returned to the dorms while Alan was lurking outside Sara's room, waiting for Gina.

Gina. Would she even want him at the Dunsberry estate now? Something told him she wouldn't let her personal feelings get in the way of business needs, yet she had moved out of her old office when Howard cheated on her. Damn that man! Because of him, Gina was afraid. Had he sounded as heartless as Howard?

No doubt about it, she was delightful to hold, a wonder to kiss...and as prickly as a cactus. Was she worth the effort?

As he blew out the last of the candles on the deck of his sailboat, he reviewed the evening yet again and decided things had been going pretty well until he kissed her. Well, he'd tried a frontal approach and been left empty-handed. Maybe what was called for now was subtlety. If he could only figure out how to be subtle when his hormones were pumping iron double time, he'd have it made.

He was in the bathroom about to brush his teeth when he came across his cranberry sweater. As she definitely seemed like the folding kind, was it an indication of how upset she'd been to leave it in a heap?

He picked up the sweater and held it for a moment, reminded of the way it had fit Gina and the way she had fit into his arms. He buried his face in the soft wool and discerned her fragrance, a cross between flowers and soap. The aroma brought back the feel of her and the wonder of her lips, the way her eyes glowed, the soft curls in her hair, the timbre of her voice, her sense of humor. Yeah, she was worth a little extra effort.

He shook out the sweater, preparing to fold it. His action dislodged something that flew across the small room, hit the wall, and landed with a crack on the tile floor. The silver locket he'd seen Gina wear each time he was with her sprang apart in four pieces.

"Damn," he muttered as he knelt to retrieve them. One was a small picture, cut to fit the oval locket. As he picked it up, he hoped he wouldn't discover that Gina was still carrying around a picture of the loathsome Howard.

He found a woman's face. She looked like a younger version of Gina, with the same reddish brown hair, the same heart-shaped face, the same large gray eyes. He scooped up the other locket pieces and the chain, which had apparently snagged on his sweater, and, standing, set all but the photo on the counter. This he held up to the bright light. On the back, he found a name and date in very tiny print. Susan Cox, 1970. Too young to be the grandmother, it had to be Gina's mother.

Well, well… Tomorrow he'd fix the locket and use it as an olive branch. With any luck, Gina would be so glad to have it back she'd forget what a jerk he'd been.

Gina lay awake in bed, staring at the ceiling. What she yearned for was an older woman in whom to confide. Grandmother was way too reticent for a heart-to-heart, and most of Gina's friends were married. While they loved to get involved in any and all romantic dilemmas, they also tended to think with their hearts and not their heads. Besides, she'd just recently given them the Howard fiasco to gossip about and she didn't feel like favoring them with anything—or any-one—new.

Gina closed her eyes and thought of Alan, allowing herself one quick moment to relive the feel of his mouth pressed against hers, the solid warmth of his body, the strength and tenderness of his hands. Obviously, the more you cared for someone, the worse it was when it was over, so it was a good thing she didn't really care…yet.

Her eyes open now, Gina flopped over onto her side. The brass lamp winked at her from its new home beside her bed. Again, her thoughts turned to a confidante, but this time, her mother's face flitted into her mind.

Gina reached for the locket and found it wasn't there. She sat up like a bolt, patting her chest, then jumped from the bed and searched the tumbled sheets and blankets. It was gone. Maybe the car, she thought, then remembered taking off Alan's sweater. She'd had it up until that time, she was sure, but once she'd torn off that sweater, all memory of it ceased.

Hopefully, he had it. Her hand reached for the telephone, then she paused. As much as she wanted the locket, she didn't want to hear Alan's voice. As there was little that could be done about it now, morning would serve, and perhaps by morning, she'd feel a little less vulnerable.

Instead of picking up the receiver, she found her hand touching the brass lamp. Even though she knew she was alone, she looked around the room before picking it up. Sara's second wish had come true. There were a dozen plausible reasons why Jason might have asked Sara to a party; the least likely was that a brass lamp had cast some spell over the poor boy. Biting her lip, Gina ran a finger along the etching, up the spout, down the smooth side so easy to rub, once, twice, three times. Again, she thought of her mother....

By Monday afternoon, all thoughts of magic lamps and long-lost relatives fled as Gina faced Julia Ann Dunsberry, detailed plans for the solarium in hand. She'd spent all of Sunday at her office, working up these plans, and now she stood, heart sinking, as Julia Ann pushed her ideas aside.

It seemed she had plans of her own. "Don't y'all love those fake rubber tree plants?" she gushed. "They've got such waxy-looking leaves, and I swear, even up close you can't tell the real ones from the phonies. I saw some at a restaurant back home that had big clusters of purple flowers dangling like grapes. Now, you can't tell me real rubber trees make flowers like that! Besides, the real ones are messy.''

Gina blinked a couple of times. Finally, she said, "But you have a gardener who will take care of the…mess. It won't be your problem." As she spoke, her mind raced—at first she'd thought Julia Ann was joking, but Julia Ann didn't joke. Then Gina's thoughts jumped ahead to what Charles Dunsberry would say when he heard his solarium was to be populated with fake plants. Her head reeled!

"I don't want the gardener mucking around," Julia Ann said firmly. "I don't like her. Her fingernails are always dirty."

"She's a gardener—"

"So, she's never heard of gloves?"

Striving for rationality, Gina said, "The solarium has an outside entrance as well as the one from inside. You'll never even know she's here."

"That's worse! No, I want *her* outside with the real plants and I want fake plants inside. Now, about the grass—"

"There is no grass in a solarium," Gina interrupted. For a second, she had a flash of someone trying to mow the lawn inside the solarium and a smile touched her lips.

"I know, I know, but I think artificial turf is so bright and pretty. We can use some here and there for effect. And I like birds."

"Birds?"

"Not real ones, they're way too messy. Just the sound of birds, you know, like in a jungle."

"I—"

"And a fountain, of course. Charles thinks the

sound of running water is relaxing. That's where we could put a cute little group of flamingos. Yes, definitely, a fountain.''

A fountain, glory be, a fountain! Gina rifled through her papers to find the one that showed her proposal for a fountain to be placed in the center of the solarium with paths leading in four diagonal directions. ''Like this,'' she said, showing it to Julia Ann. The fountain showcased was a huge circular affair she'd found in a downtown shop, made in Italy of marble with coral tiles inlaid in the basin. Gina tried to imagine it surrounded by a flock of pink plastic flamingos, but her imagination wasn't that good.

''That one is kind of boring. I want a bigger one, maybe shaped like a flower with a cute little old naked cupid.''

''A cupid,'' Gina repeated dully.

Julia Ann waved her unbroken arm. ''This will be my retreat, you know, so it has to be relaxing. Charles says I need a quiet place in nature to mend. He calls this solarium my sanctuary because I've suffered so.''

Irrationally, Gina felt a stab of guilt.

''I want a place I feel safe and secure, a place where my bones can mend. I'll need a TV out there, of course, and when I get better, I'll stick some exercise equipment in among the plants. Don't you think that would be nice?''

Gina merely nodded.

''Now all we have to do is decide on what color water goes in the fountain. I favor pink.''

Gina conjured up a halfhearted smile. ''Pink is nice. Of course, clear water is always refreshing—''

"I love pink, don't you? Y'all know this has to be finished by the Halloween bash, right?"

Gina said. "It will cost."

Julia Ann shrugged, which apparently caused her pain, for she winced next and groaned a little. "That doesn't matter."

"Thankfully the room is structurally sound. I found a new plumbing contractor who just happens to have had a cancellation so he'll be able to help us. The Briar Patch was going to supply the plants—maybe they have fake plants, as well—I'll have to check. Oh, and an electrician…friend…of mine is coming by in about ten minutes to give us an estimate—"

"Who in the world is *that?*" Julia Ann demanded, suddenly sitting taller in her chair.

Gina turned to face the same direction Julia Ann faced, which was toward the front of the house. Through the window, she saw a pickup had pulled in behind her car. Standing next to the truck, surveying the house, was Alan Kincaid.

"That's our new electrician," Gina said. She was unprepared for the jolt seeing him produced. He'd called early Sunday morning with the news that he'd found her locket, and she'd handled his call with little emotion—she'd been proud of herself—but now she was finding that talking to him over the phone wasn't the same thing as seeing him in the flesh.

He was dressed in jeans and a dark green long-sleeved shirt, his hair brushed back from his forehead, a speculative smile on his lips. At first, Gina thought he'd noticed the two women staring through the window at him, but then she realized he was reacting to another man who approached Alan with an outstretched hand. Obviously, they knew each other, for a handshake was followed with a clap on the shoulder and a quick exchange of words. The second man, one of the new plumbers, climbed in a van and drove off as Alan walked toward the house.

"My," Julia Ann said with a long, exhaled breath. "Isn't he something!"

Gina silently agreed.

"Ooh, he's coming inside," Julia Ann cooed. "Quick, Gina, how do I look?"

"Great," Gina said as she took in the orange spandex top and the yellow shorts, the pink cast and the bubbly hair. By contrast, Gina was dressed in a gray skirt and a sky blue sweater, pretty dull stuff. Good thing she didn't care.

Julia Ann fluffed her hair with one hand. "Go meet him, then bring him in here and introduce me."

Gina left the room, arriving at the front door about the same time Alan stepped into the grand entry. Up close, the impact he had on her doubled. She'd assumed she could put her personal feelings aside, but now she wondered if that would be possible.

"Thanks for coming," she said, striving to appear friendly and nothing more.

"My pleasure."

She turned, but Alan caught her arm. When she whirled to face him, she found he'd produced her locket. "I thought you might want this first," he said. He undid the clasp and held the necklace open. Gina knew the chain slid on right over her head, but it seemed kind of awkward to grab it from him, so she turned around, lifted her hair off her neck, and he fastened the clasp. She'd never before been aware of all the little nerve endings that existed on the back of a person's neck!

"Is it a photograph of your mother?"

Gina nodded. He'd mentioned the locket had broken when it fell, so she'd known he'd see her mother's picture when he fixed it. "It was taken when she was sixteen, a few months before I was born."

This response caused Alan's jaw to tighten. Was he thinking that her mother had been sent away when she was only three years older than Sara? This thought had recently occurred to Gina, too. She added, "Thanks for fixing it."

"No problem." A slight hesitation was followed by "Gina, we really do have to talk—"

"About the wiring? Yes, I know. Julia Ann would like to meet you, then I'll show you the solarium—"

"I wasn't talking about the wiring," he interrupted.

She met his gaze. "The wiring is all we have to talk about," she stated firmly.

"But Saturday night—"

She interrupted him this time. "If you want this job, it's yours. I'll do the designing, you'll do the electricity, Jaywalker Construction will construct, Roger Northern and Sons will do the plumbing, The Briar Patch will provide the plants...I hope. Anyway, I assume you get my drift?"

He leveled her with a steely look. "Yes. You're saying we'll be professional cohorts and nothing more."

Gina nodded. It took all her strength not to melt under his scrutiny. The memory of his lips and his arms was all but overpowering, but she wasn't going to let him make a fool of her again. Correction: she wasn't going to make a fool of *herself* again.

She looked down at her feet, then back at his face. "I know you're busy. If you want to bow out of this now, I'll understand."

For a second, she thought he was going to take her up on her offer. The brown eyes gazed intently at her as his mental wheels apparently spun in place. Finally, he said, "Show me the solarium."

It wasn't until then that Gina realized she'd been holding her breath. Well, that was understandable; after all, good electricians were hard to find on short notice. She nodded curtly and, turning on her heels, preceded him to the sitting room. If Julia Ann wanted to meet her new electrician, Gina supposed she'd have to make the introductions.

Alan showed no outward signs of being intrigued by Julia Ann's abundant charms. He was polite and unusually formal, qualities—along with his face and build—it was easy to see intrigued Julia Ann. After a few pleasantries, he said, "I've got another appointment all the way across town in an hour or so. I'd like to see the solarium now."

Julia Ann squirmed in her seat as much as her various injuries allowed. "Ooh, now, Alan, don't y'all run off like that! All business and no pleasure makes for a boring man. Don't you think so, Gina?"

Gina smiled carefully at Alan. She'd set the ground rules for this job, and it appeared he was going to follow them, for he barely cast her a glance. "Downright tedious," she said.

"See? Now y'all can't tell me you don't have time

for a drink. Tea, maybe, or perhaps something stronger?''

He tapped his watch. "Sorry, I really am in a time crunch.''

While Gina observed Julia Ann attempting to pin Alan down like a hapless butterfly in a specimen box, she found herself wondering about Howard. If the lady of the house had come on like this to Howard, then it was entirely possible the two of them had...no, really...that was extremely unlikely, wasn't it?

She was distracted from this fruitless yet fascinating speculation when she heard Julia Ann fairly swoon. "I've seen so few new faces since my accident," she lamented with her thickest southern accent. Patting the sofa next to her chair, she added, "A strong, handsome man like yourself could be so...helpful...around the house, I mean. Have a seat, honey.''

Alan smiled tolerantly. It was a new smile for Gina—it held none of his usual warmth, none of his playfulness. "I really have to be going," he said.

She was suddenly aware they were on the verge of losing him. Telling herself she was desperate for an electrician, and that keeping him on this project had nothing to do with personal feelings, Gina stepped closer to him and touched his arm. He fixed her with his dark gaze. "I'll show you the solarium. I'll be right back, Julia Ann."

Julia Ann's eyes narrowed for a fraction of a second as her gaze shifted from Alan to Gina and back again. Then a smile erupted on her very red lips. "Oh, I see how it is. Okay, then, you two go off and look at my little garden room. Oh, and Gina, I know you usually run all my ideas by Charles, but this time, let's keep it a secret till our big old Halloween bash.''

It was clear she'd decided the reason Alan was resisting her charms was because Gina had already staked a claim. It was hard for Gina to understand how Julia Ann could so wrongly misread the situation, but if it made her leave him alone so he could work, Gina was willing to let the misunderstanding stand.

Alan had already stridden purposefully from the room. Gina, relieved beyond words to be given a reprieve, readily agreed. "You don't have to say another word," she mumbled. "Believe me, I'll be happy to keep it a secret."

"Aren't y'all a dream!" Julia Ann gushed. Then, as she nodded toward the hall where Alan could be seen waiting, she added, "You lucky gal. Speaking of dreams..."

"Yes," Gina said. Speaking of dreams...

5

— ► —◄ —

As Alan stopped his truck at a red light, he caught
sight of his reflection in the rearview mirror. "You're
a bloody fool," he muttered. "She's going to chew
you up and spit you out." The light turned green, and
he once again turned his attention to the traffic. A
piece of notepaper on the seat beside him held Gina's
address, but he didn't need to consult it; the number
was already committed to memory.

Almost every day for the past two weeks he'd been
at the Dunsberry estate, telling himself and everyone
else that he wanted to make sure his end of the project
was done perfectly. He'd had to hire another man to
cover the apartment building his company was in the
final stages of wiring, but he couldn't imagine sending one of his men over to the estate. It had nothing
to do with work, of course; the job was simple enough
to do with his eyes closed. What took talent was
stretching it out.

What he'd actually been doing was straining for a
glimpse of Gina. Having never obsessed over a
woman before, he was unable to articulate, even to
himself, this compelling need to see her and hear her

voice. That was just as well; some things were better left unsaid and unacknowledged.

So he'd watched her work and, every once in a while, asked her a question, half the time neglecting to concentrate hard enough to actually hear her response. It was just too easy to get distracted by the way her lips moved when she spoke, the way she tilted her head as she thought, the cute little frown that would tug on her lips when she was unsure of something. And then he would nod and, acting totally disinterested in anything but his job, go back to work, wondering if she was staring at his retreat, wondering if she had been watching him, too, wondering if she even gave a damn.

He kind of doubted she did. For one thing, she seemed preoccupied by the solarium. Out of curiosity—because he figured she was mad at him so was purposely keeping him in the dark—he'd asked around and discovered none of the other contractors were very clear on exactly what was happening, either. Just like him, they'd been asked to keep what they did know to themselves. Odd.

Still, it was hard if not impossible to notice there was no fresh soil being toted in to replace the old soil that was meticulously being carted away. And what was with all the crushed rock that was being heaped onto the floor? He'd asked about special lighting for the plants and she'd hemmed and hawed and finally told him not to worry about it. Didn't she know she couldn't grow plants without proper lighting, to say nothing of adequate thermostat and humidity controls?

Alan shook his head. Right now, he didn't give a

hoot about the solarium. He was on a mission. Enough was enough. For thirteen days, he'd been practicing a hands-off approach when it came to Gina Cox. For every single one of those days he'd come close to explaining why he'd been such an oaf, how he'd followed Rob's romantic advice to appear aloof when his true feelings were anything but. He never had, though. When push came to shove, it just sounded stupid to try to blame his own foot-in-the-mouth disease on his nineteen-year-old brother.

Well, showing up unannounced like this would either work like a charm or blow up in his face, and, quite frankly, either result was better than the status quo.

The idea for his present course of action had come to him when he'd overheard Gina telling one of the plumbers what time Sunday to call her with details of the fountain delivery set for the following Monday. She'd mentioned the dinner with her grandparents that Alan had assumed had taken place the weekend before. For some reason, they'd apparently rescheduled it. This got him to thinking. Gina threw out a few numbers, Alan did some quick math, and presto, he knew what time to swoop down into her life, armed with a little bag of persuasions.

Sure enough, her car was parked in the driveway of what turned out to be a modest duplex set on a quiet side street. He pulled in behind her, effectively blocking her avenue of escape. For a couple of seconds, he sat there, and then, taking a deep breath, opened his door.

Her small porch already held an arrangement of pumpkins, corn husks and gourds even though Halloween was still a month away. A straw cornucopia filled with nuts and straw flowers decorated the door. He discovered they were all glued in place when he knocked, the door swung open, and nothing tumbled to the ground.

The prompt response was explained by the purse Gina held in one hand. Obviously surprised to see him, she slung the bag over her shoulder. "Alan? I was just leaving—"

"I know, that's why I'm here. Stand-in for ex-boyfriend Howard Raskeller reporting for duty." He saluted and clicked his heels together. He was almost sure her eyes reflected pleasure at seeing him.

"I can't believe you're here," she said. She was wearing a black dress with tiny white-and-pink flowers all over it. It hugged her bodice and waist, and flared slightly around her long legs. A hundred little buttons traveled from the hem to the neckline, which was a shade too high for his taste but was probably perfect for visiting grandparents. He found himself wishing he could unbutton a few.

"I told you I'd fill in."

"But we were only joking—"

"I was perfectly serious."

"How did you know Grandfather had a cold and we had to reschedule dinner?"

"I have spies," he said.

"Hmm—well, it looks to me like you forgot your blond wig and your sunglasses."

"I didn't grow a beard, either. It doesn't matter—the old folks will be so enamored with my dazzling personality, they'll never even notice what I look like," he told her with all the irresistible charm he could muster.

She shook her head. She was still holding on to the doorknob. He could sense she was close to telling him to get lost. Time for plan B. "Sara went to a party yesterday at a boy's house," he said casually.

"Jason?" she asked, leaning forward.

"Yeah, that's the kid. Tall and lanky, too much hair, baggy clothes. Sara thinks he's a real hunk."

There was a wistful quality to Gina's smile that confirmed his suspicion that Gina was beginning to care about what happened to his little sister. "Did she have a good time?"

"I don't know. Seemed to me she was kind of quiet when I drove her home, but she won't answer my questions, so I'm in the dark. Thirteen-year-old girls are a mystery."

Now she looked contemplative. He rushed ahead with his trump card. "I've been thinking about what you said, about Sara's room being too babyish. I was thinking that it needs to be updated. I wouldn't know where to start on a project like that, but I've been watching you at the Dunsberry house and you really know your stuff. Would you consider letting me hire you to work your magic?"

She bit her lip as she stared at him. He could tell she wanted to say yes. Question was, did she want to help Sara more than she wanted to avoid him? Second question was, would she figure out he was using Sara to get to her, and if she did, would it infuriate her or would she be flattered he'd gone to so much trouble?

"Alan, I don't think—"

He interrupted her before she could brush him off.

"You can decide about that later, but right now, we'd better get going before we're late. Your grandparents are still expecting you *and* a friend, right? I'll be the friend. You've done so much for me and mine, please, let me do this for you."

His remark about the passage of time caused her to glance at her watch, but still she paused.

He took the chance of touching her hand. "Shall we go?"

"You don't understand. Grandfather might be mostly blind, but he's lost none of his edge. Grandmother is soft on the inside but hard as nails outside. They both speak their minds, they're both demanding and gruff and say whatever they want no matter how rude or unkind—"

"I should fit in perfectly," he interrupted with a grin.

This remark elicited the first real smile he'd seen on her face since their ill-fated first date. Shaking her head, she said, "You don't know what you're getting into."

"Like I said, it's *my* turn to help *you.*"

She assessed him with dubious eyes. Heck, he couldn't blame her for being cautious, even if he was wallowing in sincerity. He grinned again and added, "I'm parked behind you. Let's take my truck. Hate to have the grandparents think you're with a man who has you chauffeur him around town."

"Heaven forbid," she said, her voice dry. Sighing, she stepped outside, locking the door behind her. "Okay, you're on, but don't say I didn't warn you."

* * *

If someone offered Gina a million dollars to tell them why she'd agreed to let Alan accompany her on this visit to her grandparents, she would have had to tell them to keep their money. She hoped it was because she wanted a Howard stand-in. She feared it was because she wanted to be with Alan.

"Turn left up here," she said. That's what their conversation so far had consisted of: directions. This was the first time they'd been alone in almost two weeks. Not that they hadn't seen each other on a daily basis, not that they hadn't spoken about the project, not that she hadn't slid him a few furtive glances when she was sure he wasn't looking. She'd told herself she would forever keep her distance from this man, that she would protect her pride and her heart from his abundant charms, and here she was, going with him to her grandparents' house of all places.

She saw him cast her a quick peek, then he focused on the road again. "So, what are their names?"

"My grandparents? Mildred and Anthony Cox."

"Milly and Tony?"

She smiled to herself. "No, Mildred and Anthony."

"Ah—"

"I told you they were hard-liners. Turn right."

After he executed the turn, he said, "I'd like to talk to you about the Dunsberry solarium."

Gina bit her lip. "What about it?" she asked tentatively.

"What's going on in there?"

"Nothing," she said quickly. "Nothing, just the usual."

He cast her a sideways glance. "The hazard of leading such an honest life, Gina, is that you never get any practice dissembling."

"Which means?"

"You don't lie very well."

"You would know," she said wryly.

He ignored her jab and continued on the topic she had always known was bound to arise. "If I didn't know better," he mused, "I'd say you were never going to put living plants in that room. I mean, there are water pipes but no sprinklers, wiring in odd places, no humidity control, and the florist seems more concerned with dust in the air than dirt in the ground. Bottom line, what's up, Gina?"

She took a deep breath. "Actually, you hit the nail right on the head." Pointing, she added, "Turn right at the next corner. Their place is at the end of the road. I'll open the gate for you."

He stopped the truck in front of the gate, but caught her arm before she could open her door. "Let me get this straight. There aren't going to be any real plants?"

"Nope. Julia Ann doesn't like them."

"What about Charles?"

Biting her lip, Gina said, "Well, Charles doesn't know. The whole thing is a secret. I wasn't going to tell anyone."

"But now I know," he said with a devious twinkle in his eye.

"Yes, now you know. So what's the price to keep your mouth shut about it?"

The twinkle deepened. "I'll have to think about that," he said.

Gina opened the door and slid to the ground, glancing back inside. "You do that."

A sexy smile curved his lips. "Oh, trust me, I will."

The tone of his voice, as well as the look in his eyes, suggested she was going to be blackmailed. Her response to this news—wobbly knees, erratic heartbeat—annoyed her almost as much as the man did.

Anthony Cox was seventy-three years old and had weathered gracefully except for his loss of sight. This condition could have been prevented if he'd followed doctor's orders when his glaucoma had first been diagnosed. He hadn't trusted the doctor, however, so he hadn't followed directions, and as a result, his vision had greatly suffered.

Near blindness hadn't changed him in any way that Gina could discern, unless you counted his occasional swing with the white-tipped cane, which seemed halfway malicious in nature. He still made his way around the house, he still listened to classical music, and he still barked orders, a habit from his navy years, which had been far behind him by the time Gina was born. He was a tall, straight man with lots of white hair and snapping blue eyes that didn't see much and yet, contrarily, seemed to miss nothing.

Mildred Cox was five years younger than her husband. She was almost as tall and almost as difficult. Gina happened to know there was a giant marshmallow lodged deep inside her grandmother's heart, and she'd often reflected how difficult it must have been for her to send her daughter away without a word, without a way home, without a hope of seeing her again. It was she who met them at the door, her spare frame covered in black polyester slacks and a black sweater, severe clothes that showcased her steely gray hair and eyes.

"You're five minutes late," Mildred said by way of greeting.

"Hello, Grandmother."

"You must be Howard," the older woman said, directing her gaze on Alan.

Gina opened her mouth to correct this wrong impression, but before she could, Alan jumped in. "Yes," he said easily. "Howard Raskeller. It's very nice to finally meet you, Mrs. Cox."

"You may call me Mildred," she said as she studied Alan's face. Gina knew what she was thinking: had the man dyed his hair and popped in a pair of colored contact lenses? For the life of her, she couldn't think of a way to gracefully contradict Alan's claim of being Howard, so she let it ride.

Alan added, "I'm afraid we're late because I was running a little behind schedule—"

"You need to learn to pace yourself, then, don't you?" Mildred snapped as she stood aside to let them enter. "After all, promptness is a virtue." Alan cast her a startled look, and Gina smiled. Well, she'd tried to warn him what her grandparents were like.

As always, when Gina came back to this house, she was struck with how Spartan the furnishings were and how bare the walls. No wonder she'd been drawn to decorating! Her hands fairly itched to have a go at her grandparents' home, but it was out of the question. Not only would they chide her for asking them to spend money on unnecessary frills, but her grandfather was used to things the way they were, which made it far easier for him to get around.

The living room was a modest square. A short vinyl couch sat against one wall, flanked by a recliner on one side and a small chair on the other. Everything faced the television set, which sat on a sturdy wooden chest in front of the window. A framed print of a navy ship provided the only artwork. There were no clusters of photographs, no knickknacks, no throw pillows. The only note of discord was the metal TV tray, which sat in front of Grandmother's end of the sofa and, as usual, held writing supplies and reading glasses.

Anthony Cox was seated in the chair, leaning forward slightly, his weight supported on the cane he grasped in his hands. His head was turned toward them. Gina knew that, backed by the light as they were, he could tell there were two people in front of him, but details would be lost. He depended on Mildred for that. Gina wondered what her grandmother would say about the discrepancies in ''Howard's'' coloring. Probably nothing.

''Come over here, boy,'' Anthony commanded.

Alan strode across the room, hand extended. ''Pleased to meet you, sir. Gina's told me so much about you, haven't you, darling?''

Gina murmured general agreement as she watched Alan try to figure out when he could drop his hand without appearing impolite.

''Shake the boy's hand, Anthony,'' Mildred snapped.

Shifting his weight, freeing his right hand, Anthony barked, ''Tarnations, woman, I can't see it!''

"It's in front of your nose!"

"Right here, sir," Alan said, grasping the old man's hand in his.

Gina held her breath, but Grandfather seemed to be in a better-than-average mood, for instead of snarling, he actually shook hands with Alan.

"Gina told us about you. You're a decorator? Hell of a job for a man."

Gina had to force herself to keep a straight face. Alan said, "Actually, I'm quitting. I'm thinking of getting into the electrical contracting business."

"You'll need training."

"I took a few classes in college. A...friend of mine owns a small business."

Grandfather nodded. "Well, at least it's a man's work. Don't you think so, Gina?"

"You know what I think," Gina said softly as she leaned down to kiss her grandfather's smooth cheek. He made a fuss as though he didn't like her doing this. The one time she hadn't, her grandmother had confided he'd been hurt. "How's your cold?"

"Gone. I won't tolerate being sick."

"I know. Grandmother, may I help with dinner?"

"A roast is in the oven. I calculate it needs another twenty minutes."

"It sure smells good," Alan said with a big smile.

"Just a pot roast," Mildred said without changing expression.

"My favorite," Alan said in such a way that it sounded true.

By now, Gina knew he had a way of embellishing the literal truth, and that anything he said had to be tempered with this knowledge. Think of the way he'd so easily assumed Howard's identity and then spun stories to go with it! But Grandmother actually produced a smile. "You two sit, I'll go check on things."

As soon as they sat, Anthony swung his cane in a low-to-the-ground arc, connecting with Alan's shin. Alan grabbed his leg and winced, but stoically, made no sound.

"So, when are you two getting married?" Anthony demanded.

Gina realized she should have known this question was bound to arise. She said, "No date, Grandfather."

"You've been seeing each other for the better part of two years! What are you waiting for?"

"There's no rush," she said calmly.

"Why doesn't the boy answer? Cat got your tongue, son?"

Alan cleared his throat. "Not at all, sir."

"So what are you waiting for?"

"Well—"

"You must have noticed the girl's getting on in years."

Gina winced, but Alan answered smoothly, "Actually, sir, no, I haven't."

"Hogwash. It's high time she had someone to take care of her."

"I don't need someone to take care of me," Gina said.

Anthony turned his head in Gina's direction. "You go help your grandmother get supper on the table and leave us men alone for a talk."

"But—"

"It's okay," Alan told her.

Gina shook her head. Even Howard wouldn't have been able to answer these questions!

"It's okay," Alan repeated.

The cane swung again, but this time, Gina noticed, Alan moved his legs out of reach just in time. "She used to mind better than this," Grandfather barked.

"Did she? Well, she doesn't mind at all anymore," Alan said with a twinkle in his eye.

She raised her hands in frustration. It looked as if they were going to discuss her like a pet canary. In disgust, she left.

Except for a couple of prolonged glances between herself and Alan, dinner passed uneventfully, which was fine with Gina. As was the custom, after the meal she always helped her grandmother with the dishes, and then they sat in the living room, watching the evening news. This had been Sunday afternoon for as long as Gina could remember, and now, as she stood in the kitchen drying familiar plates, she wondered how she'd managed to come out of this atmosphere so normal. Or was she normal? Maybe she was as odd as her family. There was a sobering thought.

She didn't even want to think about what was happening out in the living room without her.

"Last pot," her grandmother said.

Gina dried it with a paper towel and stored it in the cupboard. When she stood and took off her apron, she found her grandmother leaning against the counter, arms folded stiffly across her chest.

"I could have sworn you told me Howard had blue eyes," she said. "And blond hair. Didn't you say he had blond hair?"

"Did I?"

"Yes, you did."

"What a stupid mistake for me to have made," Gina said with a quick smile.

"Yes," Mildred said. "What a stupid mistake. Still, he's a good-looking boy. How serious are you two?"

Gina shrugged. "Not very."

"But two years—"

"Goes by so fast," she interrupted.

"I see. Why was I under the impression you were thinking of marrying him?"

"I don't know," Gina said. "Trust me, you'll be the first to know when that day comes, but it's a long way off." Figuring she might as well set the groundwork for the future breakup, she added, "Actually, we're not getting along that well. I wouldn't be surprised if it kind of fizzles out."

Mildred dried her hands on her apron. "Hmm—"

Gina, anxious to end this conversation, gestured toward the other room. "Shall we join the men?"

Mildred stared at her for a few more seconds, and then, as though turning a page in her mind, nodded. "Yes. The news is on in two minutes."

Anthony had settled down on one end of the brown sofa. Mildred sat on the other end. Usually, at this point in the evening, Mildred would dart out a terse note to one of the distant family members or friends she'd last seen fifty years before when she left Nebraska, but today, perhaps in deference to Alan's presence, she sat with her hands folded in her lap. By the way her gaze kept wandering to the tray, Gina suspected it took a lot of willpower for her grand-mother to sit and do nothing.

Alan had taken a worn recliner close to Mildred's end of the couch. As Gina passed him, he caught her hand and playfully tugged her down onto his lap, pin-ning her there with strong arms, his head behind hers.

"Al—Howard," she protested, her gaze traveling first to her grandfather, who looked annoyed by the noise, and then to her grandmother, who was frown-ing.

"Come on, honey. Let's watch the news together," Alan said playfully.

"Quiet down!" Anthony demanded as he clicked the volume higher on the TV.

Alan nuzzled her hair aside and nibbled on the back of her neck. Ignoring the molten lava that seemed to be burning its way through her body, Gina tried to turn to face him. He smiled warmly at her and kissed the tip of her nose. Gina's initial anger turned to shock. What in the world had gotten into him?

Under her grandmother's scrutiny, Gina subtly struggled against Alan's hold. Despite the awkward-ness of the timing and the situation, she found it very nice to be held so firmly, very, very nice to have his breath fall on the back of her neck, to feel him kiss her there as though they were lovers. Or maybe *nice* wasn't quite the right word for it. His hands were still clasped around her, his thumbs touching the upward curve of the bottom of her breasts. No, not exactly *nice*. Wild sensations catapulted inside her, sensations entirely inappropriate for her grandparents' home, let alone in her grandparents' presence. She smiled at her grandmother. Her mouth was too dry to actually speak.

"Considering...everything...I think this behavior is exceedingly improper," Mildred sniffed.

"What?" Anthony demanded. "What are they doing?"

"She's in his lap," Mildred reported.

"Well, they're engaged, aren't they?"

In unison, Alan said, "Yes," and Mildred said, "No."

Grandfather fixed Alan and Gina with one of his useless but intimidating stares and snarled, "One thing you should know, boy. You fool around with my granddaughter before you're married, and I'll do more to you with this cane than whack your legs, you understand what I'm saying? Now, tell her grandmother, once and for all, are you marrying the girl or not?"

The slightest of hesitations was followed by "Of course we're getting married."

Gina turned to face him again. He smiled apologetically. "Aren't we, honey?" he added.

"This makes no sense!" Mildred snapped.

Grandfather, once again, swung his cane. Instead of connecting with any of their legs, however, the cane upset the television tray, which toppled over with a clattering bang. Alan loosened his grip, and Gina sprang to her feet.

"What's all that blasted commotion!" Grandfather bellowed.

Gina expected her grandmother to shout back at him, but she was staring at her belongings, which now littered the floor. Alan straightened the tray and knelt to retrieve the scattered articles while Gina explained what had happened to her grandfather.

One by one, he set the items back on the tray. Gina saw him pause as he restacked the envelopes, which seemed to be addressed and stamped, then she saw his gaze meet her grandmother's. He smiled at her as he handed them over. "You must have a lot of friends," he said.

Accepting them, she nodded. "Yes. Indeed, I do."

"You're a very fortunate woman."

Grandmother looked directly into Alan's eyes. "I know."

Gina's gaze drifted from one to the other, not exactly sure what they were talking about.

"Will you people settle down?" Grandfather snapped.

Gina took the straight chair, facing Alan. As she stared at him, willing him to meet her eyes, he intently watched an anchorperson on the television report details of another outbreak of violence in the Middle East. It promised to be an interesting ride home.

As soon as she closed the driveway gate and climbed back in the truck, Gina snapped, "Why in the world did you tell him we were getting married?"

He shifted uncomfortably in his seat. "Well—"

"It's fine for you," she interrupted, anger rising in her throat. "They're just a couple of eccentric old people to you. You don't have to face the repercussions of all of this. You don't have to invent some stupid excuse to explain a broken engagement! What in the world am I going to tell them?"

"Actually—"

"If I tell them I broke up with you after the way you acted, they'll assume the worse, trust me. If you break up with me, they'll assume I did something so awful you had to leave." She narrowed her eyes and finished with, "What were you thinking?"

"Apparently, I wasn't thinking at all," he said sheepishly.

"That's not good enough. Do you always go around lying to people?"

"Now, that's not fair!"

"Why not?"

"You don't understand. Your grandfather is a little...well, face it, he's a little...intense. Maybe you didn't notice, but he threw some very specific threats aimed right below my waist. I was just trying to humor him."

"If you hadn't told them you were Howard in the first place, none of this would have happened," she grumbled.

"I thought that was the game plan."

"No, that wasn't the plan."

"Well, it would have been nice if you'd remembered to tell me."

She shook her head. "I just forget how easily you twist the truth around your little finger. And why did you pull me down on your lap and kiss me? Do you have any idea how much worse that made things?"

He was silent for a few seconds. Finally, he ran a hand through his hair. "It just seemed to me that we were being way too circumspect for an engaged couple. I thought it would add credence to our claim to be in love if we actually acted as though we were."

"Your claim," she corrected him.

"My claim. Listen, I'll think of something. I'll take the heat."

"You just stay away from them. Don't, I repeat, *don't* do me any favors."

"I wouldn't think of it."

"Good."

The rest of the ride was made in an uncomfortable silence. Gina was busy trying to think in terms of damage control. She didn't have the slightest idea what Alan was thinking—his thought processes were a mystery to her. It was a relief when he finally pulled up in front of her duplex. She was about to open the door when he said, "About the solarium..."

Gina had kind of hoped he'd forget all about that, but of course that was too much to ask. As the evil glint was back in his eye, she knew he was about to make some inappropriate demand, and for a second she was back on his lap, his breath teasing the back of her neck, her thoughts a frenzied melee. She finally said, "What about it?"

He hooked his left arm over the steering wheel and fixed her with a steady stare. "I've been thinking about my price," he said.

The way he said it made Gina feel faint. The cab of the truck suddenly seemed very small. She was swamped with images of his demands, and they all seemed to involve physical contact! How would she respond? Would her heart or her brain rule the day?

In the midst of all this mental confusion, Gina noticed that Alan was tapping his hand on the wheel. Egads, if he was nervous, she should probably be petrified! "What do you want?" she finally squeaked.

"I want you to help Sara redecorate her room."

Gina realized she was disappointed, but this made no sense. She wanted to help Sara, what she didn't want was to grow more intimate with Alan, and yet her disappointment felt strangely like regret that he hadn't wanted something more personal. By now, she figured, she should be a pro at juggling conflicting emotions when it came to Alan Kincaid, yet she felt as baffled by her reactions to him as always. She said, "Is that all?"

For a second, his eyes engulfed her. Then he said, "Yeah, that's all."

She stuck out her hand. "Deal." They shook hands. His clasp was warm and strong. Before she got out of the truck, she added, "I suppose I should thank you for coming with me. I realize you were only trying to help."

"Even if I did louse everything up."

"True."

"This was our second date," he said. "Did you notice I bit you?"

Did she notice! "You mean those *meaningless* little nibbles? You call that a bite?"

"I hate that word," he said.

"*Meaningless?* Well, you used it first."

"Yes, and I've regretted it more times than I care to admit."

"Funny, the power of the English language," she mused while her brain spun in circles. Was he saying that kissing her hadn't been meaningless?

"Just wait until our third date," he said, his voice suddenly seductive.

Gina blinked. "What do you do on a third date?" she finally managed to say.

"Ah, you'll have to wait and see," he told her.

"There won't be a third date," she said sternly. He just smiled.

6

Gina hurried down the front stairs of the Dunsberry estate, heavy fabric books in tow. She had one hour to get the final selection back to the furniture store, which was a good fifteen miles away. If the order didn't go in today, it would have to wait three more days, and, frankly put, she didn't have three days to waste. Time was passing—quickly, too—racing toward the time when Charles Dunsberry and all his influential friends would first gaze on the solarium.

Okay, so it wasn't the way she wanted it. Still, she was determined to do everything top-notch. If the plants were to be fakes, then they would be the best possible fakes. There would be fake flowers as per directed, but they would be subtle in execution, suggesting jungle lushness. Pink water would spurt and babble as the costliest little naked cupid in the world watched from his perch atop the fountain. The fabric she'd just cajoled Julia Ann into accepting was a beautiful watercolor flower print. And the artificial turf she'd finally settled on was more expensive than a silk carpet, and just about as soft.

She paused as she unlocked the trunk of her car and deposited the fabric books inside. Thinking of floor coverings had reminded her she was late getting to the restaurant to oversee the installation of the flying carpets. Then she needed to make three dozen calls before stopping by Alan's house to help Sara apply an undercoat to her bedroom walls. There were orders for other clients she needed to check, and she had a momentary pang of guilt over the way she'd been falling behind lately. She knew part of her problem was her preoccupation with a man she was determined to resist.

Of course, if she'd never answered that ad in the paper, half of her problems wouldn't exist. She'd still have the lamp for the restaurant owner; she wouldn't feel guilty about Julia Ann's injuries, so she wouldn't have let herself be cajoled into worrying about pleasing her. And she'd have never met Sara. She smiled as she admitted to herself that she liked Sara and wouldn't have missed knowing her for the world. And never having met Sara would mean never having met Alan....

"Gina?"

She turned toward the house. Charles Dunsberry was coming down the broad, wide stairs. His quick pace, balled fists and glum expression made clear his emotional state—anger. Gina's stomach suddenly twisted like a wet dishrag. Had Alan said something after all?

She waited for Charles to reach her side, her heart somewhere in her throat.

Grinding to a halt in front of her, Charles looked back toward the house. "I don't mind admitting I'm more than a little miffed," he said.

Gina closed the trunk of her car. She said, "I can explain—"

He paid her no attention, cutting through her excuses with an impatient shake of his head. "Trust. You know how important trust is to me? Everyone knows that about me. I'm a very fair-minded person, but I must be able to trust!"

"I know, Mr. Dunsberry," Gina said. "Believe me, I know."

"I ask you, is that too much to demand? Trust between employer and employee? Respect? What?"

"No, of course it's not too much. I'm so sorry—"

His brow wrinkled as he interrupted her again. "What *are* you sorry about?"

Gina said, "Well, the solarium, of course."

"What about the solarium?"

For the first time, it dawned on Gina that Charles Dunsberry wasn't angry with her, at least not about the solarium. This was just another example of the trouble a guilty conscience could make.

She said, "I know it's going kind of slowly and how anxious you are to have it completed in time—"

Once again he interrupted her, this time with a wave of his hand. "The solarium is between you and my wife. I have ultimate faith in her determination to see the project completed by our All Hallows' eve soiree, and I have just as much faith in your talents at persuading her to keep things—dignified. I only wish Cedric had an ounce of your loyalty."

"Cedric?"

"He's quitting. He's upstairs right this minute packing his bag. And he's blaming his disloyalty on my wife!"

Gina knew that Cedric didn't approve of Julia Ann. She'd heard via the grapevine that existed inside the Dunsberry estate that the former Mrs. Dunsberry had hired and groomed him, and that she'd been a very proper lady. Julia Ann must have come as a real culture shock.

Charles leaned forward. "He says my wife made...well, improper advances! Can you believe that?"

Actually, despite the way Julia Ann had come on to Alan, Gina had a difficult time imagining her doing the same thing with a dried-up shell of a man like Cedric. She said, "Perhaps it's not my place to say this, Mr. Dunsberry, but maybe Cedric is just trying to make trouble for Mrs. Dunsberry."

His eyelashes fluttered as he glanced once again at his house. "Oh, my," he said. "Maybe so." The speculative look hardened again into anger. "Still, the nerve, the lack of loyalty, the betrayal of trust! Julia Ann is incapacitated, acceptances are pouring in for our party, and he's leaving! How am I to run this party without help?"

Gina took a peek at her watch. She had forty-five minutes to get to the furniture store. She took a couple of quick steps toward the driver's door, wondering how abrupt she could be without offending him. She really didn't know why he was dumping all of this on her. Opening the door, she said, "I'm sure it will all work out, Mr. Dunsberry. Maybe Cedric will change his mind—"

"I wouldn't have him back, not after the way he's acted. Insulting my wife is one thing, neglecting his duties is unpardonable."

"Well, yes." Interesting priorities, she thought. She put one foot in the car, smiled briefly and said, "Let me know if there's anything I can do—"

His hand clapped down on her shoulder. For a thin man, he had quite a grasp. He said, "Smashing! I knew we could count on you!"

Gina prayed he wasn't thinking what she was afraid he was thinking.

"I'll put you in charge of entertainment. Feel free to consult the household staff for anything you might need. We're expecting about two hundred people. My, this is working out well, after all, just as you said it would."

Gina gasped. "What?"

As he explained again, she frantically sought ways to renege on what he'd taken as a firm offer of support. Didn't the man recognize an insincere conversational gambit when he heard one? What was wrong with this guy?

"Would you mind helping with the decorations, too? Jolly good! By gum, we'll show Cedric!"

Gina smiled weakly. She didn't have the nerve to deny him help, not when she knew how completely she was letting him down when it came to curbing Julia Ann. It looked as though she was now planning a party.

As Alan closed the door behind him, the sound of laughter drifted down the stairwell. Feminine laughter, soft and glittery, sweet as spun sugar, laughter that filled the heart as well as the air, laughter too long absent from the big old house. It came to him with a sudden jolt that even if he hadn't recognized

Gina's car pulled up against the curb out front, he would have recognized her laugh.

He was running late, yet he paused at the bottom of the stairs, looking upward, just listening. His step-mother had been a jolly woman, as much an extrovert as Sara was an introvert. Alan hadn't realized until just that moment how quiet it had become over the past three years. Rob was gone much of the time, Sara kept to herself. Even Uncle Joe, as impossible as the old rascal could sometimes be, was pretty sedate unless he was watching a horse race on the television, and Alan had to admit that he himself tended to go about his work without saying much. He vowed to remedy this situation, though exactly how escaped him.

He'd dropped by the house before keeping a late lunch appointment because he wanted to change into a fresh shirt. He found himself pausing at Sara's door, leaning against the doorjamb, just staring in. The room was empty now, stripped of just about everything except a ladder, a few tarps and painting supplies. Gina was atop the ladder, looking down at Sara. Rollers and brushes discarded, both of them had dipped their hands in white paint and were slapping them against the old yellow paint, leaving handprints. They began laughing again when Gina suggested they take off their shoes and do the same with their feet.

"This is a novel way to paint a room," he said.

Two pairs of eyes turned his way. Sara immediately giggled and waggled her fingers in his direction. Gina just stared at him.

"I'm going to go wash," Sara informed them, and with a last-minute attempt at smearing Alan—an attempt he foiled by ducking out of her reach—disappeared down the hall.

His gaze went back to Gina, who was now staring at her hands as though she had just figured out that descending a ladder without touching it might be tricky. He said, "You're kind of stuck up there." He didn't add that her position gave him ample opportunity to admire the way she looked in tight jeans and a clinging T-shirt.

"I don't need hands to climb down," she said as she leaned her weight against the ladder and took the first step toward the floor.

"Let me help," he said as he reached up and grasped her waist from behind. She jumped when he touched her, so he held on tighter. By the time her feet hit the floor, and he reluctantly released her, her face was flushed a lovely shade of pink. She whispered thanks as he snagged a rag from the floor and handed it to her.

"Did you get the rest of the paint?" she asked.

He nodded. "Two gallons of white paint. I picked it up yesterday after work. It's down in the garage."

"It better not be white paint," Gina said, frowning.

"It's just what you ordered, snowball or something."

"Winter Snow," she corrected him.

"That's it. Tell me, though, since when isn't winter snow white?"

"White isn't always just white," she said as though it made sense.

He laughed. "Is this a decorating axiom?"

"One of many," she replied haughtily.

He could tell she was pretending to be snotty, and

it tickled him. He'd seen a lot of her over the past few weeks. He'd seen her anxious and nervous, polite and curious, embarrassed and angry—more than once on that last one. But he couldn't ever recall seeing her so content, like a cat in a beam of sunshine, damn near purring, relaxed and happy. It was as though being around Sara brought out the child in her.

And to think if Sara hadn't forced him to place that ad, he'd never have met Gina. Maybe there was some magic in that lamp, after all!

Sara had returned, hands now clean. She pushed on Alan's back. "You're not supposed to come in here until everything is all done," she said.

He stubbornly refused to budge. Grinning at her, he leaned down, hoisted her over his shoulder and purposefully marched around the bedroom, examining every empty corner, humming to himself as Sara wiggled and kicked and screeched for him to put her down. She was laughing so hard her screams were garbled. His gaze met Gina's, and once again, he recognized a wistful curve to her beautiful lips.

He wondered fleetingly what she would do if he picked her up and carried her next door to his bedroom?

A smile split his lips at his own foolishness. Figuring out what she'd do was simple: she'd say something nasty, punch him in the kisser and bolt. Then her grandfather would come after him, swinging that blasted cane, doing who knows what untold damage to some very important body parts. Nope, better to go ahead with the plans he'd already set in motion.

An hour later, toward this end, he found himself sitting in a coffee shop in downtown Portland. Mildred Cox sat across from him, her hands folded primly on top of the menu she'd scanned briefly and set on the table. She regarded him with her gray eyes. Out of the context of her home, she seemed less formidable and a little out of place; he found himself hoping that what he was about to do wouldn't hurt her.

"Thank you for coming," he said.

She nodded. "You said it concerned my granddaughter."

"Yes." Brother, now that she was here, he wasn't sure where to start.

The waitress appeared, giving him a second to collect his thoughts. They both ordered turkey sandwiches and coffee.

Mildred tilted her head a fraction of an inch. "Does this have anything to do with the fact that you're not really Howard?"

Alan smiled ruefully. "So you knew?"

"Of course. Gina couldn't actually make a mistake about a friend's coloring. Besides, you haven't known each other for two years. That was obvious."

"Not that it really matters, but how could you possibly tell how long we've known each other?"

Her smile was as quick as a blink, gone before he was sure it was even there. She said, "You were both way too aware of each other, too nervous."

He held out his hand. "My name is Alan Kincaid, and you're right, Gina and I haven't known each other very long."

"Just long enough," she said as she shook his hand.

He wasn't sure what she meant, but he let it drop.

"I want you to know that it was my idea to pose as Howard," he said. "Gina kind of got caught in the middle."

Mildred nodded. It was hard to tell what she thought about this admission. If she was impressed with his gallantry, she sure kept it to herself. Alan knew Gina wouldn't appreciate his attempt to take the heat—she'd told him point blank not to do her any favors. He shifted uncomfortably in his seat.

The waitress reappeared with their lunch, and for a few minutes, they ate in silence. The sandwiches were huge, however, and it wasn't too long before Mildred was wrapping up her second half in a napkin.

"I'll get the waitress," Alan told her. "She can help you—"

"That isn't necessary," she said curtly. "The napkin will do fine. Okay, Alan Kincaid, lunch was very good, thank you. Now, why are we here?"

This was it, this was when he'd find out if he was barking up the wrong tree. Striving to be as forthright as she was, he said, "When I picked up your spilled mail the other night, I noticed an envelope addressed to Susan Windmere."

He detected a moment of shock in Mildred's eyes before she said, "So?"

"Susan Windmere is your daughter, isn't she?"

"Absolutely not," she said firmly.

He shook his head gently. "I'm sorry, but I just don't believe you, Mildred."

"Young man, there are many Susans in the world—"

"I know. But I don't think there are many Susans in your life living on the Oregon coast. What I want to know is how long you've been corresponding with Gina's mother.''

She stared at him for a long count of ten, then she tucked her wrapped sandwich in the front pocket of her purse. "Thanks again," she said curtly.

He leaned across the table. "Mildred, don't you think it's about time Gina had the chance to do the same thing you've been doing? Don't you think she has a right to contact her mother, maybe even to meet her? That letter was addressed to a post office box in Oldport, which is less than two and a half hours from here. Is that where Susan lives?"

For a second, he thought he'd appealed to her maternal side, but the moment passed. Mildred stood abruptly, her cheeks paler than ever, her eyes uneasy. She stared down at him, opened her mouth, then shut it without saying a word. When she left, she didn't look back.

"Damn," Alan muttered as he stared at his half-eaten lunch. He'd blown it. Either he was entirely off base about Susan Windmere being the former Susan Cox or the old lady wasn't budging on her story. But he wasn't wrong, he knew he wasn't. Her reaction had been way too strong for someone with nothing to hide.

He'd hoped to convince her to break this wall of silence surrounding Gina's mother. Face it, he'd hoped that by convincing her to do the decent thing, he'd show Gina how generous and trustworthy and loyal he was, and now he'd blown it.

He looked up when he was aware of someone standing behind him. Expecting the waitress, he pushed his plate away. "I'm finished," he said.

Mildred came around his chair and sat back down. "Maybe you're right," she said.

He waited patiently for her to decide what and how much she was going to tell him. All he wanted was to convince her to come clean with Gina, to throw the ball into her court, where he truly believed it belonged. But he sensed he'd have to go slowly.

"You're right, Susan Windmere is my daughter," she said at long last.

"How long—"

Her words came haltingly, as though she was reluctant to part with them. "I've...I've always written her. At first, we used a mutual friend...to forward our letters. Later, after Gina left home and Anthony's sight deteriorated, I wrote directly...right to her, but at a post office box, not to her home. I'd forgotten that particular letter was in the stack. I would never purposely have left it where Gina might see it...I just forgot."

"Why haven't you ever told her?" Before she could answer, he added, "Hasn't Susan ever wanted to see her daughter? How could she stay away for so many years?"

She was quiet for so long that he had time to chastise himself for pushing her. Finally, she sighed deeply. "Susan promised her father," Mildred said. "It was the condition he placed on helping her. We would raise the child, she would stay away."

Despite his intentions to play it cool, he heard himself blurt out, "But how could you—"

She interrupted him, all hesitation gone. "Young man, I am not about to sit here and defend Anthony's position! Frankly, it's none of your business. Susan accepted the terms and she kept her word, which is a lot more than most people would have done. Gina has grown up to be a fine woman with high moral values. Personally, I don't really care if you approve of the situation or not."

Alan leaned back in his chair. He said, "Then, why did you come back, Mildred?"

She studied his face. Alan wondered what it had been like growing up under that gray scrutiny. At last, she said, "I wouldn't be opposed to Gina meeting her mother. But Anthony must never know."

Alan leaned back in his chair. This is exactly what he'd hoped would happen; she was seeing the wisdom of his words, she was going to take action. "Good," he said succinctly.

"You'll have to go about it in such a way that Susan is prepared," she added.

"Me?"

She opened her purse and took out a slip of paper and a pen and jotted down Gina's mother's phone number and address. "I'll leave it to you to tell Gina, too," she said as she handed him the paper. "No one must know I had anything to do with it. Not even Gina."

"Wait a second," he said. "I'm not the one to do this—"

"Then why did *you* come?" she demanded.

He stared at her.

"You're the one to do it," she added, her voice kindlier. "I guess I always hoped someone would care enough."

"But, Mrs. Cox, Mildred, I'm not at all sure about this. Gina might resent my interfering—"

"Life is full of risks," she said.

He stared at her. What he wanted to say was that she hadn't taken risks. She hadn't stood up to her husband when her daughter was in need, and now, with Gina, she was backing down again. He wondered how she'd managed to raise a woman like Gina, who didn't strike him as someone who avoided painful situations and who by no means would defer to him or any other man.

As he sat there and grimly contemplated the many ways he was about to further mess up his life, Mildred Cox left.

Gina looked around Sara's finished room and smiled. There was something so nice about fresh paint. Sara had decided she wanted the whole room done in white. They'd refinished her furniture, painted the walls and installed new white drapes stenciled with gold stars. A decorative white picket fence acted as a headboard for a bed covered with white eyelet. There was a wicker chest beside the bed, which held a lamp covered with suns and moons, and a big old furry white area rug that cushioned bare feet. Silver-and-gold stuffed pillows were tossed casually here and there. Gina would have chosen brighter colors for Sara, hoping color would bring out some of the fire Sara kept so carefully banked, but Alan had said to give her whatever she wanted, and this was what she had wanted.

Sara was downstairs, lining up her all-male family for the big unveiling. Gina was nervous about their reactions. She heard noise in the hall, and then the door burst open and Rob entered. Sara was behind him, and Gina laughed as Rob grabbed his sister and rubbed her head with his knuckles. "Looks pretty fancy for a rug rat like you," he said.

Sara pushed herself away. "Do you like it?"

"It's white."

"No, duh," Sara said with disgust.

Uncle Joe peeked his head in. "Who in the blazes is going to keep this clean?"

"I am," Sara announced.

He shook his head. "I'll believe that when I see it," he snarled as he wandered down the hall.

"He's grumpy because his horse came in seventh," Sara informed Gina.

"I see."

Alan was last to show up. He stayed in the doorway for a second, then he nodded. "It's beautiful," he said.

"Thank you," both Sara and Gina said in unison.

As Sara showed Rob every detail, Alan approached Gina. "So this is Winter Snow. Incredible how white it looks in this light."

"Isn't it?"

He smiled winningly. "Very nice. Completely different. Sara is glowing."

"I hope you still feel that way when the bills start rolling in."

"She's worth it," he said.

For a second, they both stared at Sara, who had chosen a gauzy blue dress for the occasion and was proudly showing her new closet organizer to Rob. She looked so innocent, Gina thought, teetering on the brink of adulthood. Did Sara have any idea how lucky she was to have Alan looking out for her, caring for her needs, loving her?

Her gaze strayed to him. She'd noticed that when it came to Sara, the roadblocks between them came down. It was when things got the least bit personal that he said or did something annoying or manipulative, and then her hackles rose. It was kind of strange standing in Sara's room with Alan by her side— strange, and rather comfortable. She realized they were slowly getting to know each other on a day-to-day basis. Too bad he wasn't the kind of man she wanted to build a future with. Too bad he wasn't the kind of man who wanted to build a future with anyone!

"Are you going to the Dunsberry party?" he asked her.

"Haven't you heard? I'm the new social secretary, at least for the party. I'm in charge of games—which reminds me, I have a dozen errands to run yet today."

"Let's go together," he said. "To the party, I mean. I hate to arrive at big social events by myself."

"You're going?" she asked, surprised.

"Julia Ann invited me," he told her.

"Ah—"

"And what does that 'ah' mean?"

"You know what it means."

He leaned so close his breath teased her ear. "You think I'm planning a clandestine tryst with the injured but voluptuous Julia Ann Dunsberry?"

She laughed. "No—"

"Good. She's not only unavailable, she's definitely not my type. So how about it, do we go together?"

Gina considered his offer. It sounded innocent

enough, and she, too, hated walking into a room full of strangers all by herself. "I have to be a little early," she warned him.

"No problem. And I was thinking that as long as we're going to be arriving together, it would be fun if our costumes matched. Happens that I have a friend with a costume shop. If you're not busy Sunday afternoon, why don't we drive over there and pick out our Halloween costumes?"

She narrowed her eyes. What was going on here? For one thing, wasn't he the man who had made such a point out of telling her he didn't have the time to indulge in a long-term, serious relationship? For a man with no time, he was sure being generous. For another, Alan Kincaid didn't strike her as the party kind, yet here he was proposing a day spent picking out costumes. Interesting. "Why are you really going to this party?" she demanded.

He grinned. "Simple. This unveiling today is small potatoes next to the one a week from now. I want to be there when Charles Dunsberry gets a load of his new sanitized, plasticized solarium."

She drew back and stared into his eyes. It had been a while since she'd allowed herself this pleasure, and as always, their deep, dark depths consumed her. She said, "You are an evil person."

"I know. So, is it a date?"

"I told you, no third date."

"My mistake, I used the wrong word. Not a date, just two people driving to a store together. Kevin, that's my friend, has some really fantastic stuff. I know you'll love his shop."

Spending time alone with Alan sounded like the

best of heaven and the worst of hell all rolled up into one. She bit her lip. She wanted to. She knew she shouldn't. On the other hand, she did need a costume.

"Did I mention I have a surprise for you?" he added. "Something really special."

Gina felt herself weakening. It had nothing to do with Alan, she reasoned, nothing at all. It's just that she'd always been a sucker for a surprise.

Before Gina left Alan's house, she shooed the men out of Sara's room so she could have a moment alone with the youngster. They sat on the bed after first turning down the spread. This had been Sara's idea, and Gina vaguely recalled warning her that an all-white room with expensive fabrics would require extra care. Apparently, at least on this first day, Sara was taking the advice to heart.

"Everybody liked it," Sara said with a satisfied smile.

"Yes, you have excellent taste," Gina said.

"But you did it," Sara insisted.

Gina took Sara's hands into her own. "*We* did it. Actually, you told me what you wanted and I found it. That's what a decorator sometimes does. You can take credit for your room, Sara, it reflects you."

Sara stared at their linked hands. At first, Gina thought she had overstepped the boundaries of their friendship, but then she noticed Sara was smiling. She said, "Thanks, Gina. For everything, I mean."

"You're most welcome. Sara, have you ever heard of a housewarming present?"

She shook her head.

"It's a gift people give someone when they move

into a new house. I know this isn't a new house, but it is a new room. I have something for you.'' Reluctantly, she pulled her hands away and reached down to the floor where she'd stashed her purse under the eyelet spread, out of sight. Unzipping it, she withdrew the brass lamp.

Sara stared at the lamp, then at Gina. She looked pleased and uncertain at the same time.

Gina held it out to her. ''Don't you want it back now?''

Sara narrowed her eyes, but she didn't respond.

''See, I got to thinking about all our wishes. You with your wonderful voice getting into the choir. Julia Ann in her slippers, which probably have three-inch heels and feathers on the toes. No wonder she tripped on those narrow stairs. Then you wished for Jason, and lo and behold, he talked to you. But Sara, you're a pretty girl with a sweet personality, and besides, I bet that once you made that wish, you were friendlier to him than you'd ever been before and that gave him the courage to speak to you.''

Gina bit at her lip. ''I made another wish, quite a while ago,'' she continued, her hand momentarily brushing against the silver locket. ''It was a wish that couldn't come true, an impossible kind of wish, and sure enough, nothing happened. That's because all along, our wishes have been chance and coincidence and the power of our own convictions, Sara. This lamp is just a lamp, and I believe it's time you had it back.''

They both stared at the rich golden gleam of the brass.

Sara said, ''I don't even like Jason anymore. I went

to his party and all he did was stare at Amber. I think he talked to me to make her jealous.''

''Not a very nice boy,'' Gina commented.

Sara shrugged her thin shoulders as she took the lamp from Gina. ''It's okay. There's a new guy in class. His name is Todd. Maybe I'll wish for him!''

It was on the tip of Gina's tongue to ask Sara if she'd been paying any attention at all when she caught the faint gleam of amusement in Sara's eye. So, the kid did have a sense of irony—she was related to her oldest brother, after all!

Sara popped to her feet, the lamp clutched against her chest. Gina suddenly had mixed feelings about returning it. She'd been so sure that Sara had moved past the need for a magic lamp, but now as she watched the child carefully place it on a shelf beside her other treasures, she was filled with doubt about the wisdom of reintroducing it into her life.

Sara opened her desk drawer and produced a handful of change. ''Here you go,'' she said with a grin.

''You don't need to pay me, Sara. The lamp is just a trinket—''

''I want to pay you. I want to own it again,'' Sara insisted.

Gina could see that to protest would be fruitless, so she accepted the money, dropping it into the recesses of her purse. The lamp, once again, officially belonged to Sara.

Without warning, Sara threw her arms around Gina's neck and hugged her, then she smiled. ''Thanks, Gina.''

Gina, who seemed to find herself at a loss for words more often than not these days, nodded.

Gina settled back into Alan's truck with a feeling of déjà vu. She clearly recalled that the last time she'd ridden with him she'd sworn to them both that they wouldn't be going out together again. Maybe she should stop making these grand announcements. By now, with Alan, she must be dangerously close to having lost all credibility.

He'd picked her up right after lunch. As nervous as she'd been about the wisdom of this escapade, he'd seemed to be even *more* nervous, which was odd. Gina was willing to admit the reason she felt tied up in knots around Alan was that she was beginning to care more and more about him, and with caring came risk. She understood they could have no future together, and in weak moments, she found herself increasingly open to the thought that she might soon be willing to take what she could get. But why did *he* seem jittery?

With the completion of Sara's room and the soon-to-be finished shared project at the Dunsberry estate, their paths would likely never cross again. She looked out the window, stunned by the empty feeling this realization created in the pit of her stomach. It was obviously time for their relationship to come to a screeching halt; it looked as though circumstance was going to take care of it.

Alan seemed to be concentrating on the traffic. She snuck a peek at his profile and smiled internally. He certainly was gorgeous! His thick lashes and dark eyes, the beautiful straight line of his brows and the strong bones of his face, the chiseled quality of his lips and chin were enough to attract almost any female. Today he was dressed in a red corduroy shirt and blue jeans. By chance, she'd worn a loose-fitting red dress—they looked as though Christmas, not Halloween, was less than a week away.

Maybe he felt her staring at him, for he turned, and their eyes caught. He smiled at her, then looked back at the road.

"Gina," he said, without looking back at her, "has your grandmother talked to you this week?"

What a strange question, she thought, but she answered right away. "No. That's not unusual, though. We seldom talk unless there's something specific to say." A suspicious notion made her add, "Why do you ask?"

"No reason," he said quickly.

She shook her head and leaned toward him. "You didn't try to talk to her, did you? I specifically asked you not to."

"Calm down," he said.

This wasn't much of an answer. She glanced out the window again, trying to figure out if she wanted to know more. It was hard to see how he could have talked to either of her grandparents without making everything a lot worse. And if he had, he'd done so against her wishes, which meant she'd have to get mad at him again and she just didn't want to.

About this time, she noticed they had left the freeway and were headed west across the mountains. "Where are we going?"

"To my friend's shop."

"Where is your friend's shop?"

He slid her a quick look. "Over on the coast."

"I assumed it was in the city."

"Did you?"

Gina tapped her fingers against the seat. "Alan, what's this all about?"

"Nothing. I have a friend with a costume shop and that's where we're going. I guess I forgot to mention the shop was on the coast."

"I guess you did," she said dryly. "Come to think of it, since when does a costume shop stay open on a Sunday?"

"My friend gave me the key."

"Oh. So we'll be there all alone?"

He gave her a devil-may-care wink. "All by ourselves."

"Is that the big surprise?"

"No," he said after a longer-than-normal pause. "The surprise comes later, around dinnertime."

She folded her arms across her chest. "Alan, may I ask you a question?"

He smiled, but he didn't turn his head. "In that tone of voice? I wish you wouldn't, but I assume you will."

"You assume correctly. Why do you play so many games?"

The smile faded. "Games?"

"Yes. You've always got an angle going. Why can't you just tell the truth, plain and simple?"

"Is that what you want?"

Now his tone of voice worried her. She said, "That's what I want."

"Okay, then here's a question for you. Why haven't you ever tried to find your mother?"

His question shocked her. It came from out of the blue, as unexpected as a hurricane in a cave. After a moment to collect her wits, she answered him, living up to her own demand for simple truth. "I guess because I always figured she could find me if she wanted to and she never did. Now it's your turn. Why didn't you tell me your friend's shop was so far away?"

Another glance. "Because you wouldn't have come," he said. The way he said it and his choice of words sent a shiver down Gina's spine.

"So, I wouldn't have come," she replied. "So what?"

"So Saturday night would roll around and you'd have no costume," he said.

"I see. You were just looking out for me, is that it?"

He shrugged. "More or less. Okay, my turn. Over the years, did you ever wonder if the reason your mother didn't come back to see you was fear? Fear of your grandfather, fear of your rejecting her?"

Why was he going on and on about her mother? She herself hadn't thought much about that shadowy woman since the night she'd found her fingers rubbing the brass lamp. She had a feeling that asking him would get her exactly nowhere, so she decided to play it out. "Yes, of course I've wondered," she said. "I've also thought that maybe she hasn't come back because she hasn't *wanted* to. Maybe I'm part of a past best forgotten. Who knows, maybe one of these days I'll work up the courage to look for her. Maybe we'll be reunited on one of those daytime talk shows."

"Have you talked to your grandmother about her?"

Gina looked down at her hands. On the surface, she felt impatient with his prying questions, but deep underneath, she could feel a little spot of warmth and comfort. This was not a topic she'd shared with many people. For that matter, it wasn't even a topic she herself dwelt on. She'd been taught that the past was the past, the future was what counted, but here she was discovering that there was peace in discussing the rather remarkable events of her life and putting them in perspective.

She said, "I asked Grandmother about my mother when I was fifteen years old. She told me to let the past go, that's what my mother had done. She said to learn from my mother's mistakes and build a happy future, and she ended with a warning to never, ever ask Grandfather the same question."

There was a straight stretch of road ahead, and he spared her a longer glance. "What would you do if she showed up at your door?"

Gina shook her head. "I'd say hello," she said. Then she added, just to herself, *And then I'd tell Sara I was wrong and that she should be very careful what she wishes for on that little brass lamp!*

* * *

They found the costume shop on the main street of a very small town Gina had only driven through before. A candy store that advertised saltwater taffy was open next door, and Gina ducked inside to purchase a couple of pounds for her grandfather. He claimed it was the only decent candy made, and Gina had always thought it appropriate that an old navy man was addicted to saltwater taffy.

As Alan opened the dark shop, Gina stood in front of the window, admiring the display. "I think we'd better go inside before people see us and think the shop is open."

He switched on the lights and Gina entered, aware that he'd closed and locked the door behind her. "There's a witch's outfit in the window," she told him.

"I can't see you as a witch," he said. "Too many warts."

"I'll have you know that I happen to look rather fetching in warts. Wow, there's a lot of stuff in here, isn't there?"

They both looked around the narrow shop. It was filled nearly to the brim with suits and dresses from every time period, hats and shoes, gloves and wigs and jewelry. Every color of the rainbow seemed to be represented, and the glitter of rhinestones and sequins, the wispy plumage of dyed feathers, the sheen of satin, and the rich luxury of velvet tempted and tantalized from every nook and cranny. Racks on either long wall held all of the above, some of it stacked, some of it hanging, some of it stuffed in bins. Above the racks hung a variety of masks, which ran the gamut from cute to scary to grotesque.

"I don't know where to start," Gina said, her gaze moving from one costume to the next. Then a smile broke her face and she giggled. Pulling a leopard-print loincloth from the rack, she said, "This caveman costume is perfect for you. Come on, I dare you to try it on!"

Alan's expression went from skeptical to amused. He reached behind her shoulder and produced the feminine version of the same costume. "I will if you will," he said.

Gina cast a wary eye at the scant eighteen inches of fake fur. "I don't think so," she said.

"Chicken."

"Cluck, cluck, cluck. Okay, what else is there?"

"Pirates? Cowboys? I see a toga over there—can Cleopatra be far away?"

"This," Gina said, pulling a heavily beaded buckskin dress from the rack. It came with moccasins and feathers. She grabbed the male counterpart and thrust it into Alan's hands. "Let's try these on."

"Actually—"

"Come on," she coaxed. "I bet those two curtains hide dressing rooms. We have to start somewhere."

He smiled as though to humor her. "All right—"

Gina took her costume behind a heavy purple curtain. She slipped off her own clothes, very aware that Alan was within inches, doing the same thing, separated from her by no more than a thin wall. She could hear him moving as he first undressed and then donned the costume she'd chosen. Part of her wished she'd been brave enough to put on the cavewoman getup—seeing Alan in a loincloth might be worth the embarrassment of wearing less than she did to the beach.

"Are you ready?" he called.

They stepped out at the same time and faced each other, both of them smiling at the sight of the other. She was dressed as an Indian maiden in leather and beads and fringe, he as an explorer with an odd hat and tall boots.

He whistled. "Pocahontas, I presume?"

She touched the feathers she'd tucked into her ponytail. "You wouldn't happen to be John Smith, would you?"

"One and the same." He took a step toward her, brushing her hand with his. "Ah, but ours is an ill-fated love," he said softly.

She knew he was talking about Pocahontas and John Smith, but for a second his words seemed the embodiment of their own fate. She said, "Do you suppose they really loved each other or did she just save his life a couple of times?"

"I'm not sure. Being a romantic, I'd like to think they were star-crossed lovers."

"So be it," she said.

He ran his fingers down her cheek. "So, Pocahontas, how about a kiss or two for the road?"

His touch sent shock waves rippling throughout her body. Hoping she could come off as lighthearted as he did when her whole being was suddenly intensely aware of him, she reached up and briefly kissed his lips.

"I have to get all the way back to England on that

kiss?'' he complained. Gripping her shoulders, he pulled her toward him. ''You can do better than that.''

Gina's head was sending out a major alert to the rest of her, but the message was apparently having a hard time getting through. The pounding heart, the sudden lack of oxygen in the room, the magnetism of his eyes—all these were interfering with command signals to flee, to safeguard herself, to go as far away as possible as quickly as she could. Instead, she willingly entered the haven of his arms.

''I lied again,'' he said, his voice deeper than she'd ever heard it.

She allowed her hand to touch his lips. They were so incredibly soft. She wanted him to stop talking, to kiss her. She wanted to feel those soft lips against hers. She didn't really care if he'd lied to her. ''Hmm.''

''When I told you the reason I wanted you to come with me today. I've already made certain arrangements. The truth, plain and simple, is that I don't really give a damn what you're wearing next Saturday night, Gina. I just wanted to spend an afternoon with you.''

''I knew that,'' she whispered.

He leaned down and kissed her forehead, his mouth lingering next to her skin, his breath moist and hot. Gina closed her eyes as he kissed her eyelids and her nose, and then she felt him touch her lips with his, and she swayed. He held her tighter. Gina relinquished all control as he pressed his body close to hers and parted her lips with his tongue. He kissed her as though it was the first time he'd ever kissed anyone, or the last time, with passion that sent wave after wave of sensations cascading from head to toe.

They parted by mutual consent, each staring at the other. He kept his arms around her, one hand gently caressing the small of her back. Gina felt faint with desire. For one fleeting moment she thought of Howard, and she almost laughed. Whatever it was they'd had, it hadn't been this. She groaned as Alan leaned down and, moving her hair away with his free hand, kissed her neck a hundred glorious times before once again claiming her mouth.

The second kiss was longer, and though Gina would have wagered it was impossible to touch the first for quality, it did. She felt parts of her anatomy awakening in ways she'd always suspected they could and would and should. She kissed him back with abandon, refusing to think further than this wonderful connection between herself and a man she had gravitated toward since the first moment she saw him. Again they parted, coming up for air, reentering the real world slowly, reluctantly, breath by ragged breath.

"I'll never forget you," he said at last, his voice almost a whisper, his gaze intense.

For a moment, she was confused. Why was he telling her he wouldn't forget her? Was he going somewhere? Was he still alluding to John Smith and Pocahontas?

"I bet you say that to all the girls," she whispered back.

He raised his hands to her shoulders and took a step back. "Just beautiful Indian maidens who shake me down to my boots."

Their kisses had catapulted their relationship onto a new level of awareness, one Gina had been fighting against, and she suddenly felt the need to reassert common sense. Common sense said she was walking a tightrope by allowing this man closer and closer to her heart when his stated goals and hers didn't match. Common sense said that kissing him wasn't a good idea, that she cared too much to share any intimacy with him, no matter how small, and that each time she did, she made the rope wobble and increased the danger of a fall. She attempted a carefree smile and, keeping her voice light, said, "Well, what do you think, is this it, then? Are these our costumes?"

He looked a little sheepish. "I tried to tell you earlier. When I talked to Kevin, I asked him to put aside two particular costumes. I think they're hanging over there in those garment bags."

"Great!" she said, moving toward the area behind the counter to which he'd gestured. The first step away was harder than the second. By the time she'd taken five or six, she could no longer feel the pull of her body to his and that was a relief.

"You're right, your name is on the bags," she told him as she reached up to unzip one of the opaque plastic sacks.

She wasn't aware he'd followed her until his hand closed over hers. "Don't," he said.

She turned to face him. They were next to each other again, and the tension returned with a bang. "Why?" she squeaked.

He looked down at her with his marvelous eyes. "The truth is I think you'll balk if you see what I chose for you. I promise it will cover you decently and that it isn't rude or obscene or silly. How about it?''

"Is this the surprise you promised me?"

His brow furrowed for a second, but he said, "No, that comes later."

He was still holding her hand. Odd the way that connection resonated up her arm. She said, "Let me get this straight. You want me to blithely take this costume home and not even peek at it until I dress for the party?"

His smile was self-mocking. "I know, I know, why should you trust me?"

But she did, that was the spooky part. She shrugged. "Why not?"

"Good!" He treated her to a lazy smile. "I'm now officially declaring this our third date."

Her lips curved. "Is that so?"

"Absolutely."

"So now I get to find out what it is you do on a third date?"

He toyed around with the beads on her bodice. "It involves removing a few layers of clothes," he said.

Gina drank in the sight of his face in the dim lights, memorizing the way his features all came together to make him Alan. She ran her fingers along his chin. He caught her hand and, wrapping it around her back, drew her close to him.

She went willingly, but part of her held back, because part of her knew this moment meant more to her than it did to him. With that knowledge came a dull ache, and she knew that adding sex into an already confusing situation was a very bad idea.

Her mouth just an inch from his, she whispered, "Will you settle for another kiss?"

"Spoilsport."

In the end, he settled.

If he hadn't been attacked by a sudden case of nerves, the short drive up the coast to their next destination would have been wonderful. Gina was sitting next to him, so close her arm touched his, so close her thigh was against his. His awareness of her was so acute it made his insides ache.

He hadn't planned on kissing her, not today of all days. Blame it on the way this woman looked in buckskin, he thought with an internal smile, the way her skin glowed in those weak lights, the mysterious depths of her eyes. Blame it also on the way she'd been so willing, which had come as a very pleasant surprise.

Ah, the irony of it all. Here he'd been sneaking around plotting his flank attack, and then, on the brink of springing it, she'd capitulated right into his arms. He ran his tongue across his lips...he could still taste her. He'd had to exercise a lot of control to stop when she said stop, but now that they were embarking on this last leg of their trip, he was glad she'd stood firm. Intimacy would have made what was coming more complicated.

Might as well face it, he thought as he manipulated the curvy road that started up a steep grade, Gina was becoming increasingly important to him. He knew the party Saturday night was likely to be the last contact they had with each other unless one of them initiated something more. He knew what he wanted to happen

Saturday night: he wanted her to realize she was crazy about him. He wanted her to insist he come back to her place. He wanted her to rip off her clothes and throw herself at him!

But what about the next day and the day after that? Well, he didn't want to think too far ahead. He'd been ignoring some of his duties lately, depending on his crew to cover for him, working odd hours, depending on Rob and Uncle Joe to look after Sara. It couldn't go on forever, he knew that, but damn, didn't he deserve a break once in a while?

He felt her hand touch his leg, which sent shivers hither and yon. "Where are we going?" she asked.

This was a reasonable question that he couldn't answer. All he could do was hope Gina's grandmother had known what she was talking about. Things were moving forward now, people were involved, what he'd set in motion had attained a momentum of its own. He answered obliquely, saying, "Are you hungry?"

"Starving." He liked the new quality in her voice. It was warm and comfortable. "Is that the surprise, some cozy seaside restaurant? Hmm—I'll have scallops and shrimp and salmon and cod—"

"You're going to eat all that?" he asked with a laugh.

"And more. I'm ravenous."

They topped the hill. He'd been told it was the first place on the left, that he couldn't miss it. Sure enough, a cottage sat off the road a bit, accessible by a circular driveway. The house was small, painted dove gray with white shutters and a black front door. Barrels of asters and chrysanthemums flanked the tiny porch while huge trees dipped in the wind. The house was on a cliff, the beach down below, and from the road it looked like a postcard. Sunset was about an hour away, and Alan would have been willing to bet it would look like a million bucks from this perch high atop the ocean.

"How charming," Gina said. "Is it an inn of some kind?"

He made a noncommittal noise, acutely aware she'd accuse him of lying if he wasn't careful. He pulled the truck into the driveway and stopped by a fence that edged the grass.

"We must be the only ones here," she said, gesturing at the empty drive.

All week he'd been practicing what he would tell her, how he would tell her. He'd had the right words memorized, but now, sitting so close to her, the memory of her lips freshly burned on his conscience, he found he'd forgotten everything. He said, "Gina, this isn't a restaurant."

Her expression remained curious. "Then, what is it?"

"It's a home."

She narrowed her eyes and shook her head playfully. "Okay, I'll go along with this. Whose home is it?"

"A woman's," he said, desperately trying to remember the little speech he'd prepared for this moment. His mind was a blank.

Turning her back to the house, facing him, she touched his chin with her finger. "Are you bringing me to visit one of your old girlfriends? Rob told me you used to have them lined up out the door."

"Rob told you that?"

"You bet, and with deep admiration, I might add. So who is this mysterious woman?"

"No, no, it's not like that—"

At that moment, the front door opened and an attractive woman of about forty appeared on the porch. She was wearing a long, dark blue skirt and a matching sweater. The wind caught at her shoulder-length hair and she reached up to brush it off her face.

Alan couldn't believe his eyes—take twenty years off her, darken her hair, and you'd have Gina. Though he'd known what to expect, the sight of her standing there in the flesh took his breath away.

Gina, noticing Alan's sudden stillness, turned to look at the house. He felt her body stiffen as she gasped.

Susan Windmere, formerly Susan Cox, stepped off the porch onto the cobbled walk. She took a few steps toward the truck, and then she paused, her gaze directed right at Gina. Gina turned back to look at Alan, tears in her startled eyes, her hands trembling as she touched her mouth.

"Is she…" Gina began, but then words seemed to desert her.

"She's your mother, sweetheart," he said, the endearment slipping out. He felt a burning protectiveness building inside his chest that made him regret this surprise attack he'd launched. His plans now seemed naive and even selfish, but it was far too late to back out. "Will you talk to her?" he added.

The silence stretched on so long he was unsure what to do. At last, she said, "How did you find her?"

He'd promised Gina's grandmother he'd keep her name out of this matter, but he wasn't going to lie to Gina; he wasn't even going to stretch the letter of the truth. He said, "Honey, let's talk about these details later—you have someone waiting to meet you. Will you talk to her?"

She turned her head, and once again looked at her mother, and then she nodded. He immediately got out of the truck and held his door open for her. She slid past the steering wheel and he caught her hand, helping her down. He kept her hand in his until she took a few steps in her mother's direction and he released her.

As she walked away from him, Alan realized with a jolt that with each step she took, Gina was moving into her future; what really stunned him was the desire he had to go with her. Somewhere along the line, he'd stopped thinking of her only in terms of a prospective lover. A kaleidoscope of images flooded his head— of Gina on a ladder, of Gina laughing with Sara, of Gina looking into his eyes, blushing, of Gina touching him.

Wait a second, he was after a girlfriend here, not a mother for Sara and certainly not a companion for life!

Good thing he got that cleared up. Perhaps it was all this female emoting going on. He'd better watch himself, that much was crystal clear!

For all her life, Gina had wondered what this moment would be like. As she absorbed her mother's face, she realized she had never even come close to imagining the range of emotions that would consume

her, emotions far too jumbled and intertwined to iden-
tify.

Her mother was the first to speak. ''You look wonderful,'' she said. Her voice was like a melody to
Gina, familiar and yet foreign, a symphony of sound
that stretched back into the past and hinted toward
tomorrow.

''I look like you,'' she said.

They both smiled.

Susan gestured at the locket that Gina wore around
her neck. ''I haven't seen that in years,'' she said.

Gina covered the locket with her hand. ''Grandmother put your photo in it and gave it to me when
I was fifteen. I don't think a day has gone by since
then that I haven't worn it.''

Susan, biting her lip, held out her arms. With no
hesitation, Gina entered her mother's embrace for the
first time within her memory. Hot tears slid down her
cheeks.

When they faced each other again, Gina saw that
Susan was in much the same condition. She wasn't
sure what to say. There was a lifetime to catch up on,
details to be discovered, peace to be found...and re-
sentment to overcome. For that moment, however, it
seemed to be enough just to *look* at her.

''Let's go inside,'' Susan said at last. ''We have a
lot to talk about.''

Gina turned toward Alan. He made scooting move-
ments with his hands. ''I'll be fine,'' he said. ''Take
your time.''

She allowed herself to be led inside the cottage.

Even in her numb state, Gina could see that she
and her mother shared the common interest of interior

design. It was as though growing up in the unimaginative and semisterile environment provided by Anthony and Mildred Cox had created in both of them the need to spend their adult years beautifying their surroundings.

The house was small, but through artful handling, the rooms appeared larger than they were. The color scheme included shades of ivory, peach and aqua, and texture in both wall coverings and upholstery added visual interest. Late-afternoon sunlight flooded through a trio of huge windows in the back of the house. Susan gestured toward a twin set of barrel chairs, which were turned so the occupant could admire the spectacular view of the coastline and the ocean beyond.

Way too distracted to appreciate the view, Gina sat on the edge of one of the chairs. Now that she'd had a few minutes to adjust to the fact that she was actually meeting her mother, questions were beginning to pop into her head. As she struggled to put them in order, her mother took the seat opposite her, folding her hands in her lap.

"You must want to know a million things," she said.

Gina smiled. "Two million. First of all, do you know where my father is?"

She shook her head. "No. I lost track of him before you were even born. Mother sent me to live with some of her relatives in Nebraska after you came, and then I got married, but it didn't last. I joined the marines—just to spite my dad, I think, because I knew hooking up with any service other than the navy would drive him nuts, but of course, he never knew or cared, so what was the point?''

What was the point? Leaning forward, Gina voiced the question she'd struggled with for years. ''Why didn't you come back?''

Susan, sighing deeply, clenched and unclenched her hands, a sign of her inner turmoil. Finally she said, ''That's a tough one to answer. I was so young and afraid, I guess I thought you'd be better off without me. Besides, I promised. In our family, a promise isn't taken lightly.''

''That's not good enough,'' Gina said softly.

''Not good enough?''

''No. I grew up in the same house you grew up in, with, for all intents and purposes, the same parents. I know how impossible they can be. But time passed. You never came back for me, you never wrote me, you never tried to see me. I'm sorry, but as wonderful as it is to see you and to know you're alive, I can't get past the fact that you felt a point of honor was more important than your own child.''

''I did keep track of you,'' Susan blurted out. ''Mother and I wrote constantly. She sent me pictures—''

Gina found herself standing. ''Grandmother wrote to you?''

Susan was standing now, too. She looked contrite as she said, ''I never should have told you that.''

''Another promise?''

''Yes.''

For a few seconds, they stared at each other. Gina realized that she didn't know this woman; she was a complete stranger. They might share the same body build and eye color, the same genetic code, the same family history, but they were strangers.

Susan reached out with a shaking hand. "This is going to take time," she said. "Time for both of us. Maybe in the end you'll decide you can't forgive me, and I'll respect that if it's really what you feel. All I want you to know now is that it's like a dream come true, your being here, like a second chance to correct some of the miserable decisions I've made in my life. We'll do this any way you want, it's your turn to call the shots. That young man of yours brought us together. All I ask is that you give me a chance...that you give us both a chance."

Gina found it impossible to articulate what she was feeling. Tentatively, she took her mother's hand, met her gaze and, biting her lip, nodded. It was a beginning....

8

It was dark outside, and Alan had turned on the heater to counteract the October chill. Gina sat close to her own door. Though she'd spent an hour with her mother, they'd both barely begun to scratch the surface of those two million questions, yet she felt so emotionally drained that it was all she could do not to cry.

Alan cleared his throat. They'd driven more or less in silence for the first hour of the return trip, but it looked as though that was now going to change. Gina steeled herself.

"Are you still hungry? There's a restaurant up ahead—"

"I'm not hungry."

He waited a second before adding, "Did it...work out okay?"

Obviously, he was worried about his part in this surprise to beat all surprises. She said, "More or less."

"What does that mean?"

"It means we've agreed to give each other a couple of weeks and then we'll talk again. Alan, how did my grandmother get you involved in all of this?"

He paused. She hadn't meant it as a trick question. She added, "Don't tell me she swore you to silence, too."

"Well—"

"Honestly."

"I think she's worried about what your grandfather might do—"

Gina's laugh was slightly sardonic. "All my life, everyone has worried about what my grandfather might do or say. I love the old man, but this is getting to be silly, and I think it has to stop. I have half a mind to go over there and tell him what's going on!"

Another pause. Finally, Alan said, "Would you mind waiting until I'm not along?"

This time her laugh was as uncomplicated as spring rain. Amazing how good it felt. Eventually, she said, "Do you know that I actually wished on that fool lamp?"

"For Julia Ann—"

"No. I made a second wish. I was...well, I was kind of upset. I wished I would be reunited with my mother, and now, thanks to you, it's come true."

Even in the dim light inside the truck, she could tell he was staring at her. She suddenly felt him take her hand and squeeze it.

"I don't know exactly how you did it," Gina added, gently withdrawing her hand from his strong grasp because she hadn't yet made her point and she needed to maintain distance. "I think my grandmother must have helped you. I don't even know if I want to know how it all came about. But I do know I wish you hadn't plotted behind my back."

"Now, Gina—"

"Because this is my life we're talking about. This wasn't your problem to untangle. I told you I'd look into it when I was ready. You misled me. This is just another example of how you fool around with the truth. How can I ever really trust you?"

"Now, wait a second, that's not fair," he snapped.

"Why not?"

"Because, left to your own devices, you would have stalled forever."

"What does that have to do with anything? Besides, you don't know that I would have stalled."

"Yes, I do."

"No, you don't. You don't know me that well."

Now he laughed. "Of course I know you that well. I know you well enough to know that you would have let fear of rejection keep you from ever meeting the one person in the world you wanted to meet, and I know you well enough to know that you're using me to work out how angry you still are at the way that miserable Howard cheated on you. Once and for all, I am not Howard!"

"I know you're not Howard! And as usual, you're changing the subject."

"I am not."

"Yes, you are. Every time I get mad at you, you figure out a way to shift the focus onto me."

That got him! Silence descended into the truck, silence as thick and encompassing as valley fog. In her more rational seconds of thought, Gina reluctantly admitted the truth of some of what he said, but she wasn't going to let him know that.

As they drove into the city, Gina couldn't help but reflect on the changes this day had brought. A few hours ago, they'd been at the costume shop, trading jokes and kisses, refusing to let the future hamper a moment out of time. She closed her eyes and relived the feel of his hands rubbing the small of her back, the sensations his lips awakened deep inside her body, the feeling of safe harbor she'd felt in his arms. He'd been gentle and demanding and so sensual, and she'd known as he kissed her that it would never be like this for her with another man, never again.

And now they were at far ends of a bench seat, rattling along the highway, barely speaking.

If finding her mother was like a comet across the horizon, a comet she apparently owed to Alan, then why was she now angry with him? She thought about this as they wound ever closer to her duplex.

Her mother had said her lifetime dream was to meet Gina. Gina understood this dream—hadn't she shared it? But what next?

Family, she thought. *Somehow reuniting my entire family. Making it so my children will know their grandmother and their great-grandparents openly and without subterfuge. Holidays spent together, bad times faced and conquered, good times celebrated. That's what I want! Too much to ask for? Maybe. But not too much to work for, and certainly not too much to dream.*

And yet that wasn't all, she wanted more; in fact, she suspected that what she wanted the most might be the more difficult to attain. What she wanted in her heart of hearts was a man, a mate, someone to share it all with, someone to make the dreams worth reaching for, someone who could love and be loved without reservation. Not just anyone, either. Not a man who ran away at the first sign of trouble like her father had. Not a man like Grandfather, who insisted everything be done his way, and then demanded his wife choose between him and their child.

She wanted a man like Alan.

"What did you mean back there at the costume shop when you said you'd never forget me?" she asked him.

He spared her another quick look. "Well, you know, I just meant that no matter what happens, I'll never forget you. Damn, Gina, you must know by now that you're very special to me."

Gina nodded woodenly. She didn't doubt his sincerity, but it came to her with a dull throb that the reason she was angry with him was because she wasn't as special to him as he was to her! He'd admitted that kissing her wasn't meaningless amusement, but he'd gone no further...he couldn't. Kisses and intimacy were building blocks of a relationship to a woman like her, the foundation on which to structure a life. Alan was a kind man, generous and loving, sexy and fun, but he was a man looking for a love affair, no future, no strings. And she, heaven help her, was a marriage-hungry woman just like all the rest.

"Sara says you're coming to our house to get ready for the Dunsberry gala," he said softly.

The revelations of the last few minutes had left her shaky. It was going to be just as she'd repeatedly warned herself it would be: the longer she knew him, the harder the parting. She was pleased her voice betrayed none of these emotions as she answered, "That was the plan. Is it okay with you?"

"Of course." Again he reached for her hand, and

this time, his touch brought melancholy as Gina faced the irrefutable fact that it was high time to end this relationship. She didn't want to get into it now; he would assume she was reacting to all that had happened on this long and difficult day. Better to wait until after Halloween to tell him that, physical attraction aside, they weren't a match. It was up to her to be strong, up to her to say goodbye and then stick to it.

Sara was in a panic when Gina arrived at the Kincaid house late Saturday afternoon. "It's gone," she whispered as she ushered Gina inside the house.

Gina had the as-yet-unopened garment bag slung over her shoulder, and she was carrying a small suitcase full of makeup and the other things she thought she might need to get ready for the party. She'd spent the day over at the Dunsberry estate, attending to last-minute details. She was emotionally and physically exhausted after a week of sleepless nights spent worrying about Charles Dunsberry's reaction when he got a look at his new solarium, the integration of her long-lost mother into her life, the Halloween decorations and games, and most of all, the anticipation of telling Alan she wasn't going to see him again.

She hooked the bag over the back of a chair and set her small suitcase on the bottom stair. "What's gone?"

"The lamp," Sara said. "I've looked everywhere, I don't now what to do!"

"First thing *you* do is calm down," she told the youngster as she caught her flying hands. "Second thing *we* do is find Alan."

"He's still at work."

"On Saturday?"

"He's been working most every weekend down at the apartment complex to finish on time."

So, that was how he was handling the extra jobs— he was working weekends to cover.

"Anyway," Sara continued, "I know he doesn't have it because it was on my shelf this morning when Rob woke me up, and Alan was already gone, and now it's just disappeared."

"Maybe Rob—"

"He wouldn't take it."

Gina was alarmed at the dismay she could hear in Sara's voice. Tightening her grip, she said, "I thought you were through with magic lamps."

This remark at least got Sara to stop fidgeting. She looked a little shamefaced as she said, "I thought I was, too, and then I got to thinking that I had one more wish and I might as well make it. I've got something really important to wish for this time, Gina."

"Another boy?"

Sara shook her head. "No. Nothing like that. Besides, it doesn't matter now because the lamp is gone."

Gina released Sara's hands, inwardly chiding herself for bringing that rotten lamp back into Sara's life. "It can't just be gone," she said with a sigh. "It's got to be here somewhere. You're sure you didn't misplace it? You're sure it was on your shelf this morning?"

"Pretty sure," Sara said after a telltale pause.

"You go look upstairs, I'll look down in the

kitchen. Maybe Uncle Joe took it away again to sell in another garage sale.''

''Don't tell him about me making wishes on it!'' Sara gasped. ''He'll tease me. Him and Rob. They tease me about everything.''

''I won't say a word, I promise. Now go. Chances are it's right where you left it.''

''If it's not, I'm going to call Alan at work.''

It was on the tip of Gina's tongue to tell Sara that she shouldn't bother her brother with this while he was working, but she caught herself in time. Talk about none of her business!

''Maybe I'll call Rob first. Maybe he swiped it just to make me mad.''

''Good idea,'' Gina said as Sara dashed up the stairs. Shaking her head, she walked down the hall to the kitchen, a short trip she'd first made weeks ago. She almost expected to find Alan standing in the middle of the room, a spilled cookie tray in his hand. No such luck.

''Uncle Joe?'' she called.

No answer.

The kitchen sink was full of what appeared to be lunch dishes. A newspaper on the counter was folded to the horse racing news, its margins filled with doodles and numbers. Gina looked out the back window toward Alan's boat, which was covered with tarps, she assumed because of the weather prediction for rain. She watched the tree blow in the increasing wind, and she sighed. The house was still and quiet except for an occasional creak overhead, probably caused by Sara's footfalls.

For a second, she wondered what it would be like

to live in this house with all these people. With Joe leaving his racing forms laying around. With Rob popping in and out at all hours of the day and night. With Sara going through one crisis after the other. With Alan... Sleeping in his arms, waking with him morning after morning, sharing the evenings after long days at work, building a life, one day at a time...

She shook her head to dispel this fruitless musing. Alan had said he was building his boat because he needed something to dream about. Maybe that was the trouble—men dreamed about things—women dreamed about men!

A quick look around the kitchen produced no sign of the lamp. She picked up the newspaper. A few races were circled, a few horses' names underlined. To her, the doodles were more interesting. She especially liked the leaping stick horses and the cascading waterfall of dollar signs. A little drawing off to the right caught her eye, and turning the newspaper sideways, she was able to decipher what appeared to be a bud vase from which rose a cloud of vapor. Hmm—

Her interest was further aroused when movement in the backyard caught her attention. The edges of the tarp covering the boat were snapping in the wind. It was more than that, however, a ripple announced someone was under there. As she watched through the window, the tarp parted and Uncle Joe emerged. He looked furtively around as he began crossing the yard, one hand across his chest, a bulge beneath his sweater.

Gina looked at the newspaper again, and then back

at Joe. She opened the door, startling Joe, who met her gaze with a defiant thrust of his chin.

"Hello," she said.

"I didn't know you were coming," he grumbled as he walked determinedly past her.

"You just can't get rid of me," she joked, painfully aware that after today, there would be no reason for her to enter this house again. Closing the door, she pushed that depressing thought aside and added, "I'm helping Sara look for something."

He stopped dead in his tracks and half turned to face her. "You are?"

"It's that little brass lamp I first returned a few weeks ago, the one you sold to me at the garage sale. It's missing."

"I don't know where it is," he snarled.

She handed him the newspaper. "Don't you?"

He looked even more shamefaced. Casting Gina an annoyed frown, he produced the lamp. "Oh, you mean this thing?"

"That's it," Gina said.

He handed it to her as though the metal was hot and was burning his fingers. "Here, take it to her. What do I need it for?"

Gina gestured at the newspaper. "Maybe for the exacta tomorrow at Riverside Meadows? Have you decided to go with Bucking Betty or Speedaway?"

His expression of righteous indignation gave way to a deep chuckle. "Both, that's what the exacta is. Listen, you won't tell Sara, will you?"

"How did you find out about...it?"

"Rob heard Sara and Alan talking about a magic

lamp and wishes that came true. He thought it was funny, so he told me.''

''You don't actually believe in magic lamps and genies, do you?'' she said, chiding him gently. Brother, she was one to talk!

He stuck his hand in his pocket and produced a motley-looking rabbit's foot key chain. ''I believe in anything that might change my luck for the better,'' he said with a wink. ''Besides, I figured what could it hurt?''

Gina smiled. The rabbit's foot hadn't been so lucky for the rabbit. ''I'll tell her you were polishing the lamp,'' she told him.

He tilted his head as he regarded her, and then with another chuckle, he said, ''You know, kid, you're all right.''

''Thanks,'' Gina said. She wondered how many other people in this house were running around making wishes on an empty brass lamp.

The wind grabbed the front door and slammed it behind Alan. There was a storm brewing. All the way home, he'd seen clusters of costumed children and their parents hurrying down the road, making mad dashes up every walkway in their pursuit of treats, hoping to beat the dark and the rain.

He knew that Sara was going to her girlfriend's house for a slumber party and that Rob was at the dorm. Uncle Joe would probably go find a few friends of his own and swap outrageous stories. And him?

Well, what he craved was a very hot shower and a nap, preferably with Gina in the bed with him. Even though the Dunsberry job was done, he knew he had to find an extra hand. He was spreading himself too thin. There was a fine line between profit and quality of life, and with Sara so young, he knew which side of the line he wanted to stand on. A little extra time might mean more relaxed moments with Gina, too, a thought that helped ease some of the weariness from his bones.

A familiar stab of uneasiness assailed him as he stood in the front hallway. Gina had been acting kind of odd the past few days. At first he'd thought she'd had time to resent his involvement in finding her mother, but then he decided it was more than that. It was as though she was distancing herself from him on an emotional level, and he had no idea why.

He shook off these unproductive feelings. At least tonight, he'd be with her, and a party just might be the perfect place for them to get back on track.

He'd told her he wanted to be there to see Charles Dunsberry's reaction to the solarium. This was a partial truth. It wasn't that he wanted to see her fall flat on her face, it was that he believed she just might, and that if it happened that way, she'd need someone on her side—enter him. When he'd accepted the invitation from Julia Ann he'd still been plotting the back-door strategy to win Gina's heart and, truth be known, other juicy parts of her anatomy, but now those motives seemed outdated and he wasn't exactly sure why.

Sara raced down the stairs, and he caught her with one arm as she attempted to turn the tight corner to head for the kitchen. She looked up at him, and Alan felt his mouth drop open. "Sara?" Her lips were ruby red, her eyelids blue, her brows dark, and a black mole sat saucily by the corner of her mouth. She was wearing a red cotton peasant blouse and a full flowered skirt tied around her waist and hip with a scarf.

"I'm late, Alan, let me go!" she squealed.

"What's going on?"

"Caroline made it a costume party at the last minute. Gina is turning me into a gypsy. I found Mom's old wig but we need some beads and more scarves and stuff. I'm going out to the garage to look in that box above the washing machine."

"It's storming out there," he said. "I'll bring you the box."

The doorbell rang as Sara thanked him and dashed back up the stairs. Alan called for Uncle Joe as he found the candy dish and treated the kids at the door. Uncle Joe took over door duty as Alan dodged the first raindrops and found the box Sara wanted. He carried it upstairs, very aware he was running late.

"Here's your box," he said as he entered Sara's bedroom. Gina was standing behind Sara, fitting a curly black wig over his little sister's fine gold hair. Gina was wrapped in a flowery kimono, her coppery locks loose on her shoulders. She looked good enough to eat, bite by delicious bite.

"I'm sorry I'm late," he told her.

"It's no problem. I finally smarted up and hired four people to run the Dunsberry show, so tonight I'm a guest like everyone else."

"Except for when you open the solarium—"

She shook her head. "Please...don't remind me of that."

Sara had wiggled out from under Gina's hands. She looked so different with makeup and wig that he wasn't sure he would have recognized her if he'd passed her on the street. As he watched, she tore the lid off the box and dipped her hands into her mother's treasures.

"Look at these," she said, lifting a strand of bright green beads. "And these...and these."

"They're wonderful!" Gina said.

Alan touched Gina's arm. "Have you seen your costume?"

"No. I've been too busy with Sara to even peek at it."

"Give me fifteen minutes to take a shower and change clothes. I'll meet you downstairs."

"I don't know that I can put on a costume in so short a time—"

"Trust me, you won't have any problem, there isn't that much to it."

Her eyebrows shot up her beautiful forehead.

He left in a hurry. He didn't want to be anywhere within slapping distance if she didn't like what he'd chosen.

Gina unzipped the garment bag with trepidation. At the shop, after those memorable kisses, she'd been willing to go along with Alan's little game, but now in the cold light of day, figuratively speaking, she wasn't sure how wise it had been to be so complacent.

Oranges and yellows and rusts greeted her eyes. Sheer layers of filmy, transparent nylon. A bra and panties made of a blessedly opaque gold velvet. Gold shoes with turned-up toes. Sparkles and glitter, tassels and ribbons.

"You're going to be a genie!" Sara cried. "That's perfect!"

Alan was absolutely right. There wasn't much to the costume. "I can't wear this," Gina gasped.

"Sure you can. Try it on."

She stared at the yards and yards of transparent material. Not having given it much thought, she hadn't known what to expect—she only knew this wasn't it! "I should have brought an alternative costume. I can't believe I let him talk me into trusting him."

"Just try it on," Sara repeated.

Gina closed herself in the bathroom attached to Sara's room with a connecting door and donned the costume. The undergarments, more like a two-piece bathing suit than underwear, turned out to be generously cut and edged in sequins. The pants, which rested on her hips, were made of nylon in a layer of each color. The layers were tied at the ankles with ribbons, then slit to the thighs. The top had billowy sleeves, tied at the wrists, slit to the shoulders, open down the front until it tied at the waist. She laughed at the partial image she could see in the small mirror and, opening the bathroom door carefully, peeked out to make sure Sara was alone. What she saw froze her in place.

Sara the gypsy was standing by her bookcase, brass lamp in hand, eyes closed, head bowed. Her words, though spoken in a whisper, were perfectly audible to Gina.

"So this is my last wish, my third wish. I want a mother. Not my own real mom, I know she's in heaven. I want...Gina." Sara rubbed the lamp.

Gina carefully closed the door and leaned back against it, one hand clutching her stomach, the other covering her mouth. She felt faint with alarm. She'd been so busy worrying about falling in love with Alan, focusing selfishly only on herself. She'd never stopped to think that maybe Sara was spinning fantasies of her own! Wonderful...impossible...fantasies.

Sara knocked on the door. "Alan just went downstairs. Are you ready, Gina?" Her voice sounded light and airy and full of hope.

Gina swallowed the lump in her throat. She took a second to compose herself, then answered, "Just a moment."

"Hurry."

Merciful heavens...she would have to have a heart-to-heart talk with Alan *and* Sara, she realized. But not tonight. Tonight was fraught with its own perils. There would be time enough tomorrow to face reality. She opened the door and conjured up a smile—a feat worthy of any card-carrying genie.

Sara clapped her hands together. "That looks great, Gina, it really does."

She was still so rattled by Sara's wish that she stood there, momentarily confused.

"It covers everything, honest."

The costume! Gina looked down at her veiled limbs. "Does it?"

"Sure. Look in my mirror, you'll see."

Resolutely putting aside her worries about Sara, Gina looked in the full-length mirror. Well, it left very little to the imagination, that was for sure, but the multiple layers did obscure some of her curves. She quickly ran a brush through her hair and decided to leave it down on her shoulders—she needed all the coverage she could get.

"Put on the shoes," Sara prompted as she dug through her mother's box. Gina put on the fanciful gold shoes as Sara produced a large pair of gold hoop earrings. "How about these?"

"Perfect. Thanks. I'll come over here tomorrow afternoon and return them. Maybe we can talk."

Sara grinned as she withdrew a long rust scarf. "This matches, tie it in your hair. What are we going to talk about?"

For a second, Gina just stared at Sara, trying to remember when this new bolder child had chased the timid little mouse away. She shook her head and answered, "We'll think of something."

"Okay."

Gina wound the scarf through her hair with lots of advice from Sara, then she stood, reminding herself to suck in. Thanks to Alan, she'd have to remind herself of this every fifteen seconds for the rest of the night.

"One more thing," Sara said as she retrieved the brass lamp. "Your third wish!"

They both turned as Alan's faint voice called out Gina's name from downstairs.

"I don't have time," Gina protested.

"Yes, you do. Please?"

Gina did not want to make any more wishes, never, never again, not on brass lamps or coins in a fountain or candles on a cake. But Sara's blue eyes were imploring, and she found she lacked the will to deny her this one small favor. "Oh, all right. Give it to me, I'll make a wish, but just because you want me to."

She was rewarded with a smile, which prompted her to brush aside the stiff black curls and kiss Sara on the forehead. "I want you to remember that you and I are always going to be friends," she said with feeling.

Beneath her garish makeup, Sara looked half pleased by this mushy sentiment…and half embarrassed. "Make your wish," she coaxed. "It's your last wish, so make it special."

Gina took the lamp and closed her eyes.

"Wait!" Sara cried. "You have to pay me, it has to be yours."

Again, Alan's voice called out, but this time it sounded closer, as though he was coming back up the stairs.

Gina pointed at her purse. "Dig a dollar out of there."

As Sara did so, Gina closed her eyes again. Alan's face filled her mind. She found it wasn't difficult to make this wish, not at all. She wanted him, she wanted him to want her. And not just for an hour, or a week, or a year… As her fingers rubbed the brass, the futility and heartbreak of it all made her head swim, for it was a wish, just like Sara's, that couldn't come true.

When she opened her eyes, she found that Sara had left and in her place was Alan, dressed all in white, like an Arabian prince, with full trousers and a cape. Gold braid ran down his legs and across his chest, and his head was wrapped in a swath of flowing white fabric. With his black hair and dark, dark eyes, he looked the part of a hero—her hero. He also looked incredibly sexy, and the expression in his eyes as his gaze traveled her body made Gina intensely aware of every single molecule—and how little there was covering them!

He smiled, which made her heart thud in her chest. "Are you making wishes again?" he asked teasingly.

If wishes were only heroes, she thought fleetingly as she put the lamp down on the dresser and commanded her voice to betray none of the emotions which were bombarding her from every quarter. "I was just appeasing your little sister. Where is she?"

"She went off to my room so she could talk to her girlfriend in private. Didn't you hear the phone ring?"

Gina stared at the extension that sat by Sara's bed. She hadn't heard a thing, which she found rather startling. Of course, she'd been preoccupied with thoughts of Alan and magic lamps. She said, "Funny how much more there is to your costume than there is to mine."

"You look absolutely perfect," he said, his voice soft and deep.

"I look like some kind of male fantasy and you know it."

"Hard to dispute that. Turn around, let me see the back."

"I have a feeling everyone will be seeing everything before the night is through. I don't suppose you want to loan me your cape?"

"And ruin that look?" He held out his arm. "I believe we're way past being fashionably late. Come, you bewitching genie, it's time to go."

As she moved toward him, she said dryly, "I suppose I now have to call *you* Aladdin?"

With an exaggerated leer, he took her hand and folded it over his arm. "*You* can call me Al," he said, with a glint in his eye. When he leaned down and lightly touched his lips to hers, Gina finally acknowledged to herself that it was too late to protect herself...too late to avoid falling in love. The best she could hope to accomplish now was damage control!

9

Gina faced two hundred strangers. Four hundred eyes, all turned on her. Three hundred and ninety-eight if you subtracted Alan's eyes, but she didn't want to do that as his were the warmest.

Charles Dunsberry, dressed as Napoleon, stood on one side of her, and Julia Ann, her empire-cut gown covering the cast on her leg, sat in a gaudily decorated wheelchair on the other side. They had just announced it was time to present the newly refurbished solarium.

Charles glanced down at Gina, who was suddenly very aware of her costume—or the lack of it. His eyes seemed a little more lively than usual. "Do you want to say a few words?" he asked.

Gina met Alan's gaze. He winked at her. She said, "No, I think the room can speak for itself."

The three of them, along with a selected group that included Alan, made their way toward the double doors that provided the interior access to the solarium. A ceremonial orange-and-black ribbon had been draped across the closed doors. Charles pushed his wife's chair close to the ribbon and handed her a pair of scissors.

Julia Ann cut the ribbon. Charles then pushed both doors inward.

Due to climate controls, the room was warm. It was also filled with the sound of birds, a regular cacophony of them. Junglelike, the silk plants and trees and bushes rose on either side of a brick path, so lushly, and with such beauty, that even Gina was momentarily awed. Three dozen varieties of flowers, some of which had never really existed, peeked through the leaves, showing splashes of pinks and yellows, reds and oranges. The real showstoppers were a trio of palm trees laden with coconuts, which looked real enough to inspire dreams of piña coladas. And over the entire room was the sound of running water, gurgling and splashing, not from one fountain but three, all different, all beckoning.

Gina was very aware no one said a word as they moved toward the center of the room. As she was ahead of everyone else, she couldn't see their expressions, but she could feel the tension as people must have begun to discover that the velvet green grass was actually more closely related to velvet than to grass, and that the plants, down to the last twig and petal, down to the acrylic drops of dew on the broad leaves, down to the occasional spider or butterfly crawling, hovering or flying, were phonies. Well, there went her career....

She turned at the central fountain, which was the largest. Three four-foot-high pink metal flamingos twisted and turned around each other while water gurgled up between them and splattered down into the pool in which they stood. Around them, grouped for conversation, were clusters of chairs and love seats, upholstered in a watercolor print, and glass-topped tables. Garden carts were filled with potted silk flowers, carved and painted parrots perched high atop eight-foot wrought-iron stands, and a truly magnificent life-size bronze sculpture of a lioness and her cub added points of interest. While water splattered and splashed behind her, she finally met Charles's eyes.

He looked stunned.

Julia Ann tapped Gina's arm. "Where's my pink water and my cupid?"

"Down that path," Gina said, pointing to the north. "There's another fountain, a private fountain. I call it the romance nook, and it's very private."

Julia Ann winked. "Clever girl," she said softly, and then, clapping her hands together, added in a louder voice, "Don't y'all love it!"

Gina's gaze strayed to Alan, who seemed to be absorbing every detail of the lavish and slightly ridiculous room around him. He finally noticed her stare and, flashing her a smile, gave her a thumbs-up gesture.

Gina smiled in return. No matter what Charles thought, Alan approved, and she was stunned at how much it meant to her. That sensation almost immediately gave way to one of dismay....

However, Julia Ann's enthusiasm was contagious. As she sat center court, wave after wave of guests dressed in costumes ranging from pirates to belly dancers to ghosts to movie stars came through. Many took off down one of the other three paths, where Gina could hear them call out to one another as the terrain and the "plant" life changed, and they discovered private sitting areas, additional fountains, still pools of acrylic water and stone animals tucked into unexpected places.

Alan disappeared into the throng, leaving Gina more or less alone with Charles. She took a deep breath. "I know this isn't what you expected," she said.

He rocked back on his heels. One hand was tucked beneath his jacket in true Napoleonic style, the other rubbed the back of his neck. "You're right, it isn't," he said.

Gina had known all along that she was going to disappoint him, and now she wished he would shower her with threats, threaten to fire her, anything but look so contemplative.

It was on the tip of her tongue to assure him all the substructure was in place for a complete renovation of the renovation and that she wouldn't charge him an extra penny to tear it all out and start over again, when he added, "This room has my wife's name written all over it."

She didn't want to start blaming Julia Ann.

"Let me tell you something interesting," he said, his thin lips breaking into an even thinner smile. "I didn't interfere with or even care much about what you and Julia Ann did to this room because I'm allergic to most plants and all birds and never dreamed I would actually enter it again after tonight."

"I didn't know—"

"Of course you didn't. But Julia Ann did. Don't you think it was rather sweet of her to insist you create a garden room I could enjoy, too?"

Had she? Gina wasn't about to admit that she had

a hard time seeing Julia Ann worrying about anyone else's reaction to just about anything. She said, "Very sweet. And she was quite adamant, too."

He nodded as his eyes began searching for his wheelchair-bound Josephine, and Gina felt a twist of envy in her heart. She wanted to be free to look for Alan like that, free to think he worried about her and cared about her, free to worry and care about him. As strange as the Dunsberry's relationship was, at least they had each other. After tonight, she wouldn't have even that much.

Those who wanted to bobbed for apples in the huge entry. Gina had organized this game at the last minute and with reluctance because she couldn't imagine a lot of well-heeled society types would want to dunk their heads in a bucket of water. Julia Ann had insisted, however, and as Gina watched, a senator dressed like Calamity Jane did her best to nab an apple.

Other games and amusements were being played out all around the downstairs floor of the huge house. Waiters with trays laden with champagne and the fanciest food Gina had ever seen made their way between groups of revelers. Given orders to decorate with both English and American traditions in mind, Gina had banished bats and ghosts and witches to the outside of the house. Inside the front hall and throughout the interior, she'd used a harvest motif with gilded sheaves of wheat, garlands of fall leaves and flowers, wreaths festooned with polished apples and nuts, pumpkins and gourds, strings of black lights, and legions of huge white-and-gold candles to suggest bonfires. The candles cast strange shadows on the high walls—they also reminded Gina of Alan.

She didn't like the way thinking about a man she was in love with made her feel hollow and sick in the deepest part of her stomach. How long would it take to get over him? She had no idea. No way could she use her experience with Howard as a guide. In retrospect, Howard had been a safe bet, a man she could pretend to love without having to invest any emotional energy in actually loving. Howard was to her what she was to Alan....

From the front sitting room, she heard the cheers of a group playing a game Charles remembered from his childhood, which involved a flour cake and a sixpence. A large room toward the back of the house had been emptied of furniture and now boasted a trio of circus tents, which in turn housed fortune tellers, complete with crystal balls and directions from Gina to keep the predictions happy.

Gina looked around for Alan, whom she hadn't seen since they'd been in the solarium. Maybe Julia Ann had cornered him, maybe she should try to find him. For a second, she recalled his thumbs-up, and she smiled to herself. Without warning, she felt tears building behind her eyes, and she swallowed and blinked to stem their flow. She felt profoundly sad that this love was going to founder, that she was going to be the one to scuttle the boat, but she had to look out for herself and for Sara and, really, truth be known, for Alan himself. She willed the tears away as the next game was announced.

Hesitant to face Alan until she had her emotions under control, Gina decided to stick around and see how it went. She'd had a hand in organizing this game, too, and despite her mood, she was curious if it would work.

A woman dressed as Little Bo Peep was the first to take a chair, settled there by an actress made up as a hag. She was given a small mirror, and as the hag recited doggerel that predicted what the lady's husband-to-be would look like, the room went black. A single shaft of light shot across the room from a point high on the stairs. It hit a reflection point, which sent it beaming into the mirror the woman held. She gasped in delight as a man's face appeared in her mirror!

Gina smiled. She knew that up on those stairs, behind a temporary divider, were a couple of good-looking actors with enough disguises to satisfy the hopes of a hundred single women. There was also a gorilla mask and a few stuffed animals, just to keep it fun.

She watched this game for a few minutes before Charles Dunsberry showed up by her side. "Smashing costume," he said in his clipped way, then he gestured at the empty chair. "Now then, you next."

As there was no graceful way to refuse him, Gina allowed herself to be seated on the chair. The hag leaned close. "Abracadabra," she whispered, sending a chill up Gina's spine. "Who shall it be? Who is the man who will marry thee?"

The lights went off. Gina held the mirror. The shot of light from above bounced off the reflector and the fuzzy stuffed face of a panda appeared in her mirror. She laughed, but as she did so, the panda disappeared, and Alan's face snapped into focus.

Gina stood abruptly, dropping the mirror, where it shattered on the floor. The lights went on. Someone said something about seven years' bad luck. Someone else said something about finding another mirror so the game could continue. Gina barely heard any of it, for she had turned toward the stairs and was watching Alan descend.

Their eyes caught. He grinned at her. Gina slapped a hand over her mouth and, turning, fled the room.

He found her in the solarium, but it took some looking. She had secreted herself away on a small bench toward the northern corner. A fake banana tree and a couple of ferns crowded the bench. She was staring down into a still pool.

"Gina?"

She jerked, obviously startled by his voice. For a second, he just stared at her. All evening he'd been drawn to looking at her, and it wasn't just because of the way she was dressed, either, though he would have been happy to peel her, layer by transparent layer. He sat down beside her.

"I didn't mean to upset you," he said, taking her hands into his. "I was coming down the stairs when I saw you sitting on that chair. One of the actors said I could stand in front of the light."

"It's okay," she said, staring at their linked hands.

He kissed the top of her head. It was his plan to take a bevy of kisses further south toward her mouth, but suddenly, she raised her head and met his gaze. "We have to talk," she said.

There was a quality to her voice that shook him,

that scared him. Her eyes looked miserable. He waited.

"I can't go on like this," she mumbled.

He wasn't immediately sure what she meant. He said, "Like what, Gina?"

"I can't see you anymore," she said, lowering her gaze.

He felt a stab of panic, but immediately comforted himself with the knowledge that she'd said this before and yet here they were. On the defensive, he snapped, "Is this because you think I lie?"

She bit her lip. "It's not that. I know your motives for elaborating have always been selfless. I know that I was overly sensitive because of Howard."

"My motives weren't always selfless," he said, correcting her. "However, they were never intended to cause you pain."

"I know," she whispered.

"Then, it's because I found your mother and surprised you. Do I need to remind you that you're the one who made that wish on the lamp—I was just a hapless pawn!"

He realized his weak attempt at humor hadn't worked when tears spilled over onto her cheeks. "Your life is so full," she said. "You don't really need...me...."

As her voice trailed off, he wondered what in the hell she meant. He made himself wait until she continued. "Alan, be truthful. There's no room in your life for...me. We're not a match. It's best if we part now because—"

He couldn't stand to hear another word. Pulling her into his arms, he kissed her for all he was worth. He kissed her hard and long, willing her the whole while to recognize the honesty of their kiss, to awaken her feelings for him and to understand the depth of his feelings for her. He kissed her in the hope she'd come to her senses.

For a second, he thought it had worked. For a second, she relaxed in his arms and she was his, but in the next breath, she pushed herself away from him, out of his arms, onto her feet, and without looking back, hurried down the path, a lithe figure in shades of autumn, walking out of his life.

The panic returned, but this time it wasn't a stab, it was a throbbing ache. He tried to think. She wasn't angry with him. So why was she leaving? Things had been going along so perfectly!

Her words came back to him. She'd said his life was full, there was no room or need for her. This was crazy! How could she kiss him like that and not sense the extent of his need for her?

For some seconds, he sat there, elbows resting on bent knees, staring into a pool filled with fish that never moved. It took him forever to realize the fish were fake. The water was fake, too! It was a pool of plastic that looked real enough to wet a man's feet.

He shook his head. What a talent this woman had! In this room, with Sara, over him. What a woman she was, what a love.

She thought he didn't need her, that his life was too full. She was echoing his words, made at the beginning before he'd been blindsided. Notice the way she hadn't said *she* didn't need *him*, that *her* life was too full for *him*.

It came to him slowly, painfully, almost, because awareness meant leaping gigantic, self-placed hurdles.

"She's in love with me," he finally whispered, and her moodiness of the past several days suddenly made sense.

He laughed, but abruptly stopped. The fear this knowledge awakened flamed and burned and turned to nothing more than a warm ember in his chest. He was suddenly aware of rain pounding on the roof. The storm had arrived.

This time, he found her trapped within a rowdy circle of people who'd probably had a glass too many of the excellent champagne Charles Dunsberry poured. Her face was tear-streaked as she fought to make her way to the front door. As lousy as the weather outside was, it appeared as though she was getting ready to go out into it without so much as her coat.

He shouldered his way through the crowd, unhooking his cape as he moved. When he finally reached her side, she looked up at him with eyes that cut right through to the center of his soul. He saw she was shaking; instinctively, he knew this condition had nothing to do with the temperature. He draped the cape around her shoulders, anyway, and leaning down, whispered in her ear.

She couldn't hear him, information she relayed by shaking her head. Alan looked around the room, but it was too crowded and noisy to think straight. With a smile, he leaned down and lifted Gina into his arms.

She immediately threw her arms around his neck as she studied him with bewildered eyes. Poor, poor darling. Here she'd made another attempt to leave him behind, and he was going to ruin it. He carried her through the crowd, which quieted down as they passed, casting them amused glances. He took her to the bottom of the stairs, away from the noise, and then he put her down.

They stared at each other. He realized that the next few minutes would seal his future, and that decisions made in the height of emotion were seldom trustworthy. And then he realized he'd made this decision weeks before, that it had just taken his head a while to catch up with the rest of him.

"I love you," he said simply.

He thought she'd like knowing that, but instead, it caused more tears to puddle in her gray eyes. She shook her head.

Yikes, had he misinterpreted what she was trying to tell him? He added, "Don't you love me, too?"

Without pause, she said, "Yes," but her voice trembled.

"Well, don't sound so happy about it."

"Oh, Alan..."

Nodding, eyes narrowed, he put a hand under the cape, grasping her bare shoulder. His thumb rested at the base of her throat, her pulse pounded. For one eternal second, it was as though their very life forces were joined, as though her heart beat for him, too.

"I get it," he said, his voice husky. "It's not enough that we love each other, is that it?"

Blinking, tears rolled down her cheeks. She nodded.

"You want marriage," he said. "You want to be Sara's mom. You want to live with me. You want me to love you like no woman has ever been loved for the rest of your life. And when we're old and gray and living on our tiny little sailboat, you want to tell our children about how stupid and dense their doddering old father used to be, how scared he was of claiming the woman and the love and the life that he wanted more than he wanted his next breath. Is that it?''

She stared at him for a long time before she nodded. Since she couldn't know exactly where he was going with all of this, he realized she was afraid to move any farther out on a very precarious limb. He leaned down and kissed her, a salty kiss to be sure, but a kiss that inflamed him from head to toe. This was his woman, she would be there for him and, by God, he would be there for her.

Gina cupped his face with her slender hands and drew away. "What exactly are you saying?" she asked, her voice shaky.

"Don't you know?"

"Say it," she whispered.

Smiling, he caught her hands in his. "I'm saying that I will throw myself off a mountain if you won't marry me. Will you, Gina? Will you marry me?"

She sounded incredulous—and frightened—as she squeaked, "Are you sure?"

"Oh, God, Gina, don't make me go through my life without you. You do love me, don't you?"

She nodded. New tears were moistening her eyes.

"Say it."

She blinked the tears away. "I love you. I don't know how it happened so fast when I told myself over and over again that it mustn't, but it did. For better or for worse, I love you from the very depths of my heart, and yes, of course, yes, I'll marry you."

She folded their hands back against her breasts. The warmth that pulsated through her skin into his just about drove him nuts. Only their lips met, and the kiss, less aggressive than the others, held a note of promise that a kiss had never before held, at least not for him.

"I made a third wish a few hours ago," she whispered at last.

He smiled. "And what did you wish for?"

"I wished for you to love me."

"I never even stood a chance," he said. In the back of his mind, it occurred to him that the lamp was at the house, and since Gina and Sara were finished with their wishes, maybe he could give it a whirl....

"Three wishes, all of which came true," she said, staring right into his heart. "Imagine that."

That's when he knew he didn't need a magic lamp...he had Gina.

"Imagine," he said.

* * * * *

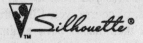

Share in the joy of yuletide romance with brand-new
stories by two of the genre's most beloved writers

DIANA PALMER

and

JOAN JOHNSTON

in

LONE STAR CHRISTMAS

Diana Palmer and Joan Johnston share their favorite
Christmas anecdotes and personal stories in this
special hardbound edition.

Diana Palmer delivers an irresistible spin-off of her
LONG, TALL TEXANS series and Joan Johnston crafts an
unforgettable new chapter to **HAWK'S WAY** in this wonderful
keepsake edition celebrating the holiday season. So
perfect for gift giving, you'll want one for yourself...and
one to give to a special friend!

Available in November at your favorite retail outlet!

Only from

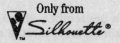